CHRISTMAS
Out of the
ADVENT BOX

Reclaiming Christmas for Fun, Faith, and Family

BY
BENJAMIN R. HUSTED
& his family

Published by

V M I PUBLISHERS

Partnering With Christian Authors, Publishing Christian and Inspirational Books

Sisters, Oregon

www.vmipublishers.com

ISBN: 1-933204-28-1

Library of Congress Control Number: 2006929962

Author Contact: bhusted@valornet.com

Table of Contents

Introduction

How does a family keep a Christmas season centered upon Jesus Christ with activities that not only strengthen the family but are also fun at the same time? This is a question millions of Christians ask every year, often without finding a good answer. Our family has discovered at least one good answer, and we would like to share it with you.

Beginning with our son's second Christmas, we have prepared for Christmas for over twenty–five years now by celebrating the season of Advent with a wreath and a modified Advent calendar that we call the Advent box. Behind the box's doors that represent consecutive days of the season of Advent are adventures for the family to do together, such as a story to read, a puzzle to solve, or a special activity—from eating a meal in silence to delivering homemade breads to neighbors. Whatever the exercise may be, each one is centered on Jesus Christ and brings the family together with cherished traditions.

Why do we Christians give presents at Christmas? Why do we put up a tree? Why do we use so many lights? What place does Santa Claus have in a Christian Christmas? These, along with many other questions, are answered day after day as we open "the box" to see what the devotion for the day is all about.

Our family—Dad (Ben), Mom (Judy), three children (John, Joy Lin, and Rebekah) and daughter-in-law (Missy)—shares with you in this book what we have done to create a Christ–centered Christmas season for ourselves. Written mostly by Dad, with short essays, recipes, and devotions by other family members, this book is arranged in three convenient sections. The narrative chapters in Part One discuss how we became involved with this unique celebration of Advent when our first child was born and the surprising development of the memorable tradition that we now love. The four chapters of Part Two provide a variety of devotions, including ones regarding the background of our well–known American Christmas traditions. Part Three consists of several appendices for those who want to know more about some of the subjects we treat only briefly, including good stories, books, and videos to enrich the season. We also have included detailed instructions for those who want to make an Advent wreath or their very own Advent Box.

The devotions in Part Two—a dozen or so for each of the four weeks of Advent—can be used right from the book and will provide lasting spiritual benefits for your family. Just "opening the box" and using them without preparation, however, is not the way to get the greatest value from this section. Instead, you should take the devotions prayerfully from the book, adapt them to the life and times of your family, put them in your own Advent Box, and enjoy the adventure!

If you are looking for a celebration of Christmas that goes beyond the shallow and expensive secular box and strengthens your family by focusing on Jesus Christ, accompanied by lots of adventure and laughter, you have come to the right place! Read on, and be ready for the Holy Spirit to give you wonderful ideas of your own as you see how we do *Christmas Out of the Advent Box*.

Chapter One

Where Was Christ in Our Christmas?

Our daughter Rebekah once said that sometimes around Christmas our neighbors must think we're crazy. "Out of the blue," she said, "we'll light a campfire in our yard and eat outside in below–freezing weather. We bake bread and take it around to church members and even neighbors who never go to church. We go *caroling*. Who *does* that kind of stuff?"

Indeed, there really is a method to our apparent madness. For more than twenty–five years now, we have counted off the weeks before Christmas by using our Advent box. Our three children have grown up with the box and cannot remember when they did not have it around to show them the richness of the season. The story of how the box came to be used in our family dates back to the earliest years of our marriage.

Judy and I were getting our own first–hand education in family living. Our first–born son was ten months old. John was crawling. He was walking. He was running! He was eating our house plants, along with their potting soil. And, he was sucking up knowledge like a huge vacuum hose! We were literally running to keep up with him.

As Christmas approached, we wondered what John would learn about it. We realized that his education would come through his wide–open eyes, inquisitive ears, the taste test and, possibly, breakage! Of course, he wasn't going to learn a lot about "Christmas" itself; every day was special and unique to him since he was seeing everything for the very first time. For him December 25 would be just another day in a whole lifetime of unique days filled with new sights and sounds.

But what would the next Christmas be like for him? And the next? When he was six years old, would Christmas be just a jumble of family, food, gifts, Santa, Rudolph, Frosty, and "Jingle Bells"? When he turned sixteen, would the traditions surrounding Christmas be only a bunch of silly stuff trying to distract him from the increasingly expensive gifts? At twenty–five, would his main concern be "the economic impact of the holiday shopping season"? Or would Jesus Christ, King of kings and Lord of lords, be the center of his Christmas?

Judy and I were committed Christians. Jesus Christ was, and still is, the center of our lives. It wasn't until that first Christmas as parents, however, that we really began to look at the traditional American celebration of Christmas and wonder where Jesus was in all of it.

Since our first Christmas together, Judy had been talking about developing our own Christmas traditions that we would do together as *our* family to draw us closer together and define who we are. Her very large extended family had enjoyed many traditions together, including cutting down a cedar tree off their own land, participating as the main family in the Christmas program in their little country church, and eating Christmas dinner at Grandma and Grandpa's with all thirty–seven cousins. They were poor enough on their farm in the hills of Oklahoma, but they were rich in their traditions!

My side of the family, in contrast, had few traditions. We had moved away from our all of our extended family in Kansas because of Daddy's ill health when I was six years old. He had almost died during boot camp at the beginning of World War II due to a relapse from rheumatic fever. His illness left him with a damaged heart, which left him physically unable to cope with the heat and humidity of eastern Kansas. So, he and my mother decided to move to a dry climate where he would be more healthy. The move worked out for him, because in Los Lunas, New Mexico, he was as healthy as the proverbial horse. He started a dairy farm and worked as hard as any man ever did.

But there, on our dairy farm, all the traditions we had known in Kansas were nonexistent. It never snowed on Christmas Day and our family was hundreds of miles away. The Hispanic culture in New Mexico was foreign to us, and the overwhelming presence of the Catholic church, so different from our midwestern Protestantism, left us feeling isolated—without traditions. We did buy a tree off the lot at the very end of the season, when prices were slashed and only a few poor ones were left. We did have a few decorations, such as our manger scene made out of clothespins and scraps of cloth. On Christmas morning, we each got a stocking holding ribbon candy and an orange, along with some good presents like socks and pajamas and sometimes something special, too. Then we went out to do the chores—just like every other day.

So when Judy began to talk about "our traditions," I really didn't know what she meant. But I began to see that traditions—those things we do over and over again together—actually form and define the substance of each individual family. My family, with its few traditions, was not close–knit, while Judy's was very close. Because I was accepted into her family and liked that type of togetherness, I worked with her on our traditions.

The first traditions we developed, such as they were, however, seemed to fit in with those all around us in our culture, which were becoming more commercial, more trivial, and less identified with Jesus Christ every year. So when John was born and we started looking at Christmas with fresh eyes, we knew we wanted something different, something richer, and something more authentically Christian, but we had very little idea what that would be. We were simply just like the rest of the American culture in that department. We had a tree and lights, gifts and a manger scene, traditional foods, and a trip "home" for Christmas. Our church presented a Christmas program about the birth of Christ, and then Santa made a "surprise" visit, giving everyone candy and fruit.

Judy and I wanted some other traditions that really centered on the Christ child, but that was all we knew at the time. We didn't even know anyone to go to for advice, because everyone we knew did the same things we did for the most part: what everyone did! We were lost! So we made this a matter of prayer. During that first Christmas season as parents, we prayed and talked, and listened and read, expecting to receive some answers to our confusion. We were not disappointed, for we began to sense the Holy Spirit giving us two very surprising answers.

First, He softened our hearts, drawing us toward a tradition championed by the "liturgical" wing of our denomination, which was not easy for Him to do. In fact, it was a miracle of no small measure! As fairly radical Christians, we wanted our experience of faith to be fresh, new, and immediate—not mediated through any form or symbol.

Judy had been raised in a small, independent, rural, Pentecostal church. Her pastor had founded more churches than I have served in as pastor, but he did not use any liturgy, symbols, written prayers, special clerical clothing, or formalities.His emphasis, instead, was just on singing, praying, preaching, and getting a fresh touch from God! The first time Judy attended a denominational church was after we got married, and she had no familiarity with—and saw no need for—what the "liturgy buffs" championed.

I grew up, on the other hand, in a very traditional church where we followed certain rituals because we always had done it that way. We were a bunch of dairy farmers who didn't know much about religion, but we did know "that's the way we do things." I don't know about the rest of them, but I grew up without a relationship with Jesus Christ, never really "hearing" the Gospel—possibly through no one's fault but my own.

In college, however, while still active in the denomination of my childhood, I had a very powerful, dramatic experience of salvation and the baptism in the Holy Spirit. Transformed by the power of God, I had all the zeal of a convert! Suddenly, I understood that Christianity was so much more real than any church traditions I had known before, and I wanted everyone to have that same intimate relationship with Jesus Christ. Following my conversion, I spent four years in seminary pressed to defend biblical Christian experience against those who believed that tradition, liturgy, or social action—rather than a personal relationship with Christ—was the heart of the gospel. Those years left me with some understanding and appreciation, along with suspicion, regarding the other positions, yet with no less zeal for mine.

As you can understand from our particular backgrounds, anything less than a personal experience with Christ was an immediate question mark for us! The people in the "liturgical" wing of our denomination were always concerned about forms, symbols, colors, written prayers, and traditions—all of which were instant turn–offs to us. So when I say the Holy Spirit softened our hearts toward "something championed by that wing of our denomination," I mean that He performed a miracle of some magnitude! Although not a dramatic miracle, it involved quite a revolution in our spirits.

God used the lively, faith–filled members of the church I was serving as associate pastor to do this. (It is wonderful how churches educate pastors!) We watched these people add something called an "Advent wreath" to the Sunday morning worship service in preparation for Christmas. They were able, along with the gentle promptings of the Holy Spirit, to get us beyond our objections to see the purpose of the Advent wreath: to present Jesus Christ.

We quietly decided that the Advent wreath would become a part of the celebration of Christmas in our home, so we adopted this new family tradition.

The second answer the Holy Spirit gave us was the Advent box. This is really what empowered us to center our Christmas season on Christ. The box is a tool by which we build the season day by day, but it depends upon the main visual expression of Advent: the Advent wreath.

In Judy's Words...

I have always loved Christmas! Some of my favorite childhood memories are about Christmas traditions. We ate Christmas dinners on the big back porch at my grandparents' because there wasn't room for all thirty–seven of us cousins inside the house! The Christmas play at our little country church told the same story and had the same characters and songs every year, but it never lost its excitement. The Christmas sacks everyone received after the program were filled with an apple, an orange, and a clump of (usually already–stuck–together) old–fashioned hard Christmas candies.

So when Ben and I began our own family, I was eager to help him find ways to make Christmas special for our new family each year. With Christ being the center of our lives, we wanted Him to also be the center of our Christmas season. In addition to that, we wanted to have family–centered traditions that would bring us together at Christmas instead of more activities sending us flying in different directions. It was also of major importance to me that it be fun, something our children—and I—didn't feel obligated to do just because we were Christians or a pastor's family. I didn't want our children to grow up feeling they had lost out on the fun of Christmas because it was Christ–centered. Instead, I wanted the season to be something extraordinary because it *was* Christ–centered.

During the first Christmas season after the birth of our first child, John, we came across an article concerning the season of Advent, the Advent wreath, and an Advent calendar. Ben was vaguely familiar with the tradition, but it was all new to me. Was this something we could use for family devotions? We began studying and brainstorming, and the ideas grew and grew. By the next Christmas, Ben—the builder he is—had conceived the idea of "the box" and designed it himself. I started looking for box fillers, and, when the Advent season arrived, we were off on an exciting spiritual journey that has lasted for twenty–five years. We have watched our children grow, from the excitement of "it's my turn to open the door" to the challenge of filling some of the cubbyholes and doing the devotions themselves. Now we find it rewarding to watch them use the box in their own homes.

Although I led some of the devotions every year, my main job was keeping everyone's schedule on hand and planning a period of time each day that we could sit down at the table and enjoy a meal, each other, and the daily devotion. The box also became a year–round adventure, as I found myself collecting ideas all the time. I was always on the lookout for new stories we could read or new recipes to try, and sometimes while shopping I often found myself looking for just the right tree ornaments or objects to put in the cubbyholes.

This will be our first Advent as empty nesters. No doubt the cubbyholes will have some of the same objects and stories that they've had in them for twenty–five years. And we'll probably "guess what's behind the door" while laughing and enjoying them and playing "remember when." But now we can also tailor the box for the two of us. We will enjoy some activities that the kids never would have, or do things for each other and people in our community that we never had time to do because of the busyness of our kids' lives. But just as in years past, I find myself looking ahead; only now I'm thinking, "Oh! Wouldn't that be a neat idea to put in the box to do when the kids and grandkids come home?"

Yes, I love Christmas, along with the traditions we have built around the box. I have also discovered the box makes a wonderful storage place for all the tree ornaments! Next season, pull out the box, and all of your ornaments will be there—unbroken. That's a nice tradition, too.

Chapter Two

God Was at Work in Another Age

We had adopted a new tradition: to celebrate the season of Advent, not just Christmas, we would use the Advent wreath. It was not radically important to us that we understand all the origins and meanings of Advent or all its traditions and symbols, but that we could fight against the commercializing and trivializing of Christmas. We absolutely did not want the season defined by the reminder, "only twenty shopping days left until Christmas!" Nor did we want Christmas, "The Festival of Christ," to be buried under tinsel, snow, and silver bells!

Here is a season closely identified with the traditions of the church, the body of Christ. So, according to the church, it is not "twenty shopping days..." Instead, it is (in 2006), "Monday of the first week in Advent." It is a matter of deciding who sets the rules and calls the shots. The economy that laments about "another disappointing shopping season" does not define the season for us. Expensive gifts and elaborate parties do not characterize the season; fortunately, Santa and Frosty do not make the rules. What we desired instead to emphasize in our celebration of Christmas was rejoicing in the coming of Jesus Christ to this earth, welcoming Him into our hearts afresh, and looking forward to His second coming! We continue to be thankful that the Holy Spirit led us along this path to find such a gem of a tool—in what we thought to be the most unlikely place.

Though it was not terribly important to us that we know everything about Advent, we still needed to know *something*. What the Holy Spirit did in answering our prayers was to give us—who valued the Bible and our personal experience with Jesus Christ above all other things—respect for a structured and solid tradition that developed during the period between the writing of the New Testament books and before the dawning of the twentieth century.

All we knew about those centuries was that they were the Dark Ages, when the Church became a powerful and corrupt institution, only to be rescued by the glorious Protestant Reformation. Of course, it wasn't that simple. The Dark Ages weren't totally dark, and the Reformation wasn't altogether glorious. Those centuries were filled with people like you and me, with families like yours and mine which were loved and loving, tried and torn, victorious and sometimes vanquished. They were times just like ours during which one generation of those who confessed Jesus Christ sincerely wanted to pass their faith on to the next generation.

One of the tools the Holy Spirit led our predecessors in the faith to develop was the church year, or the church calendar, to ensure that the full gospel of Jesus Christ would be proclaimed every year. With a definitive church calendar, local pastors, often poorly educated themselves, would not get so caught up in one aspect of the gospel that the next generation of believers missed other important points. This calendar (see Appendix Five for details), which divides the calendar year up into six (sometimes seven) seasons, provides a way for local churches to address the major elements of the gospel, including the incarnation, life, death, and resurrection of Jesus; the gift of the Holy Spirit; personal repentance; and our growth in grace.

This system works quite well in many ways as long as real faith is practiced. When faith dies, however, the whole calendar becomes just a dead form. Unfortunately, many of the clergy and laity alike, not realizing anything is missing, defend the dead form as if it were the real thing. Judy and I were, and still continue to be, opposed to this practice of dead religion. What the Holy Spirit did was let us see that the season of Advent on the church calendar might really become—as it was intended to be in the first place—a servant to our faith.

Advent is the first season of the church year, a special time to celebrate the coming of Jesus Christ, welcome Him into our hearts, and look forward to His second coming. Although these three elements of His coming have been essential building blocks of our twenty–first century faith, we were actually surprised to discover that they were all included in the meaning of this "liturgical" season.

This Advent season, in preparation for Christmas, has always ended appropriately on Christmas Eve. Its beginning date and length, however, were a little more difficult for us to grasp. The season always begins the fourth Sunday before Christmas, which varies its length from year to year. If Christmas falls on a Sunday, then Advent will be twenty–eight days long, because the fourth Sunday before Christmas is a full four weeks prior to the day. However, if Christmas happens to be on a Monday, then Advent will be only twenty–two days in length. Thus, the last week, the fourth week of Advent, may be as short as one day, or it may be a full seven days, which can be confusing!

In celebrating the season of Advent, the most common visual symbol is the Advent wreath, which we had decided to adopt as a traditional part of our family's preparation for Christmas. This wreath can be as simple or as elaborate as you desire, but it must have four candles placed around the perimeter and one in the center. These four candles, as you might have guessed, represent the four Sundays—or weeks—of Advent, and the one in the center is called the Christ candle. On the first Sunday of Advent, the first candle is lit. On the second Sunday, that candle and another are lit and so on until all the candles are burning, including the Christ Candle, which is lit on Christmas Eve.

The tradition, for reasons that I never discovered even though I did want to know, gives the four perimeter candles these names and meanings:

- First, the Prophecy candle—planning
- Second, the Bethlehem candle—preparation
- Third, the Shepherds' candle—sharing
- Fourth, the Angels' candle—joy

Whatever the origin of these meanings was, when we followed the right order we discovered a very nice flow to the season: God planned for Christmas, then the prophets announced this plan; He made preparation for the incarnation, centered in Bethlehem; the shepherds shared what they had seen and heard; and the angels announced, "Joy!" These elements provide a framework for addressing the entire Christmas story, as well as one for the celebration of Advent: plan for Christmas, prepare for it, share it, and rejoice! Remembering that the fourth week can be as short as only one day, you will see that the "rejoicing" only lasts for one day in certain years, but it is always followed by Christmas Day, which is full of joy.

This much of the tradition we discovered to be fairly universal, but other details we found to be more fluid. There are, for instance, several traditions concerning the colors of the candles. The colors assigned to the individual candles are not the "gospel truth"; rather, sincere Christians have developed different traditions over the centuries to help them *tell* the gospel truth. When we realized this, we saw that there is no exactly "right" or "wrong" way to set up the Advent wreath—despite what strong advocates of one tradition or another may contend. With this new flexibility, we tried several traditions before settling on one that worked well for us. (Other traditions are listed in Appendix Four.)

We use four red candles around the perimeter of the wreath and one white candle in the center for the simple reason that these colors are easy to find. We weren't looking for ways to make the season more difficult! We try to buy good candles with color all the way through them; the "dipped" candles tend to burn too fast and their outer layers are too easily chipped off. Also, good candles burn completely, rather than melting all over the wreath!

We had adopted a tradition, but we still didn't have a wreath. As we thought about making one, many practical considerations had to be addressed, which resulted in a unique design. First, we wanted real evergreen branches in our wreath; if it was supposed to symbolize life, we didn't want plastic. Second, we wanted to design a safe wreath, which was a challenge, considering we had small children. Third, trying to shape real evergreen into the shape of an actual wreath over and over again (because it dries out and begs to be replaced) did not seem like fun! Finally, most of the designs we read about were for temporary wreaths with Styrofoam bases and that kind of thing. We wanted a wreath that would last a lifetime!

THE ADVENT WREATH AS THE CENTERPIECE FOR
OUR CHRISTMAS EVE DINNER

The Holy Spirit graciously answered our prayers by giving us some wonderful ideas for what became our very own unique Advent wreath. What we created, as you can see in the picture, is a "two-tiered" wreath made of wood. The base is plywood, cut in a circle, and the upper tier is two 1x2 boards about eight inches long, fitted together at right angles. Toward the ends of these boards and in the center, holes are drilled to insert the candles. The two tiers are separated by dowel rods inserted into the base and the bottoms of the boards, so that the top is about four inches above the base. This lets us simply lay freshly cut cedar (abundant around eastern Oklahoma) on the lower tier, filling the space full, while keeping the branches away from the burning candles. We can easily change it every few days without trying to tie it together into a wreath! That may be cheating, as far as a wreath goes, but we don't have to please anyone but ourselves!

This wreath has been the Advent centerpiece in our home for over twenty-five years. The traditions surrounding our Advent wreath provide a structure to our preparation for Christmas and direct us to remember and re-present the Advent of Christ. The Holy Spirit graciously gave us the plan for our wreath, and He will give you a design for yours if ours does not suit you and your family. What is important is that your family develop your own traditions to keep Christ as the center of Christmas.

So, the tradition in our family is lighting the candles on the wreath for our noon meal on Sundays and usually for the evening meals for the rest of the season. We light the candles and then ask, "Who wants to open the door?" The door is in the box, which was the Holy Spirit's other answer to our prayers!

In Joy Lin's Words

"I get to open the box tonight!" sang Joy Lin.

"Nuh–uh...It's my turn. You opened it last night," Bekah retorted.

Knowing he had a better idea, John played it cool. "Fine, but I get to light the candles."

Welcome to Advent season at the Husted home. It would probably be nice to say that this conversation only took place when we were kids, but the truth is that it stayed the same for the most part until we moved away from home. By that time, we were mature enough to only think, "I want to open the box really badly," and actually say, "John, why don't you open the box tonight, since you haven't been here." It has always been good–natured, and we never were mean about it; it is just such a coveted thing to open the box.

We love the anticipation of being the first one to crack open the door, peek inside, and then leave everyone else in suspense. Was it the bell? (Of course, it was the bell. It was the first day of Advent, wasn't it?) Was it the box of matches signifying *The Best Christmas Pageant Ever*? Was it the orange Christmas light, telling us to get in the car and drive around looking at lights, only to come home and say (every year), "Oh, wow, look at that house. Those are the most beautiful lights we've ever seen!"? Only Dad knew what was to come, but what we knew was that it would be something good. Even after all these years, we still have that same childlike anticipation about the secrets in the box.

Sometimes I try to decide what my favorite box devotion is, but I never can. I pick one, but then remember another and change my mind. I love the stories because Dad is such a great reader and does voices, and we have collected so many really good stories and books. I love eating in silence like the biblical figure Zechariah because it is such a challenge for us to not talk at the table. I love making gingerbread houses out of graham crackers and watching everyone's house fall apart just when they think they are home–free. (And, may I just add, I love the laughter we inevitably share over Dad's houses. I hope he puts a picture of them in here for you to enjoy, as well.) I love just about everything that comes from the box.

As we kids got older, Mom and Dad decided it was time that we started planning some of the activities in the box. One night I was reading the Christmas story and got to the part where everyone had to go back to his birthplace to pay taxes. All of a sudden, this idea popped into my head! Where were we from? Germany, once upon a time. So my devotion for the box during Bethlehem week was a German–themed meal, as best I knew how to prepare the food. It was so fun! We had little place cards with our names and a German flag on them. We had pork chops, sauerkraut and potato salad. (You can do what I did... Get on the Internet and search for German recipes.) Now that I'm writing this, I think I should have added one more thing: everyone had to pay taxes to me. That would probably not have gone over well.

So what does the box do for me? Why do I love it so much? Simply because it brings us together; it's a connection we share. Last year Bekah found copies of *Santa, Are You For Real?* online and bought one for John, Missy and me. I think that was the best present I got last year, not because it was big and beautiful or cost a lot (I think she spent a dollar on mine), but because it was so...us. It's not just a good story anymore. Because it was in the box every year and we all sat down after supper to listen to Dad read it, that simple story represents family to us kids.

The box does not have to reveal some big spiritual truth; it just has to bring the family together. That, in essence, is what the box means to me...family.

Pork Chops and Sauerkraut

2 (16–ounce) cans sauerkraut
4 to 6 center cut pork chops

Place sauerkraut in casserole dish. Trim fat from pork chops.
Lightly brown pork chops and place on top of sauerkraut. Bake at
350 degrees for one hour.

German Potato Salad

6–7 medium russet potatoes
½ pound bacon, fried and crumbled (reserve 2 tablespoons fat)
½ cup celery, chopped
½ cup onion, chopped
1½ tablespoons flour
½ cup water
⅓ cup vinegar
⅓ cup sugar
1½ teaspoons salt
¼ teaspoon pepper
½ teaspoon celery seed

In large pan, cover whole potatoes with water and cook until tender/firm. Remove from heat; pour off water and cover with cool water. When cool, peel and cube, place in a large bowl and add the crumbled bacon. Sauté celery and onion in the 2 tablespoons bacon fat for one minute. Add to potatoes and bacon. In a saucepan, mix flour and water and stir until smooth. Stir in vinegar and cook, stirring constantly, until thick. Remove from heat and add sugar, salt, pepper, and celery seed. Mix well, pour over potatoes and toss lightly. Refrigerate and let rest overnight. Reheat salad in a casserole or serve cold. It's good either way.

Chapter Three

The Holy Spirit's Other Answer

One year, my parents had given Judy and me a subscription to Guideposts magazine. Actually, the giving of magazine subscriptions as Christmas presents had become a tradition for my parents; it was something they could do without going shopping, and they could give each of their children, along with their spouses and children, gifts suited to their individual interests. Most of the articles in Guideposts were—and still are today—light and interesting stories of people from many walks of life who find inspiration to live out their faith, providing moments of encouragement for readers. One particular article in the December, 1978 issue was highlighted by the Holy Spirit like it had a beacon on it or a crowd of angels standing around cheering and pointing to it. After reading and re–reading the article, I shared it with Judy. We studied its ideas together, realizing, "This is what we have been looking for!"

In the article, actress Mala Powers described her experience with the same dilemma we were facing concerning Christmas, and her way of addressing it with success over the previous twenty years. When her son was very young, she had also wanted to create a family tradition to make Christmas less commercial and more full of the love and truth of Jesus Christ. We were impressed that she had been concerned about this problem in 1958, a time that we thought of as far simpler than ours in 1978. As she struggled with this issue, someone gave her an Advent calendar, "a large, decorative card with little window flaps that opened to reveal pictures underneath, one for each of the 24 days of Advent," as she described it. One little flap was to be opened every day of the Advent season to reveal a picture of some element of the Nativity scene. She explained how she had, at first, just talked to her son about each picture, soon discovering that their discussions led to a special time of devotion and family closeness that had been missing from past Christmas seasons. Her article went on to tell how, over the years, she developed and collected stories to go along with each little picture until she had a whole season of special stories that she shared with her son. Then her son told his friends about these stories, and they came to their home to hear the Advent devotional every night. When she wrote the article, her son was already grown and had left home, but some of the neighborhood children still came over every night before Christmas to listen to her Advent calendar stories!

That was exactly the kind of thing we were looking for—one that would give us a simple, child–friendly devotional for each day of the season. In 1978, we couldn't find a single Advent calendar anywhere. Today, I went online, surfing the Net for "Advent Calendar." My search was as quick as the click of a mouse, resulting in a "hit list" of more than 485,000 entries. As you might imagine, the variety of calendars you can order online is amazing! There are antique calendars, calendars with chocolates, quilted calendars, calendars with Santa or New England themes without any reference to the Nativity, and even a Perl calendar with a Perl programming utility for each day of the season!

In fact, many of those calendars represent exactly what our family was trying to avoid: the trivializing and commercializing of the season. Furthermore, most of the calendars offered are not actually designed for the unique dates of the Advent season, which varies in length, but have been standardized for the twenty–four days of December preceding Christmas. While this makes the mass production of calendars easier, it misses the point of Advent; unfortunately in our society, commerce, mass production, and standardization have set the standard, not the church of Jesus Christ. Finding what you are really looking for today—with nearly half a million choices, and many of those doing the opposite of what you want to do—may take longer than it took us in

1978. On the other hand, many of the calendars are very interesting, creative and beautiful; at least you will enjoy looking at the variety and surely find something of interest.

For better or worse, 1978 was long before the Net, so our search took much more time and was mainly limited to our denominational resources and the local Christian bookstore, neither of which offering any Advent calendars for sale. We could find Advent devotional books for adults, along with books about Advent and the Advent wreath, but not a calendar. Because the idea developing in our hearts came from the Holy Spirit, however, it did not go away, for it held too much interest and promise to simply fade out of our memory. So, our dream for an Advent calendar was placed on the "back burner" of our minds, where it simmered and gained flavor as we prayed and thought. True to the usual workings of the Holy Spirit, the idea grew and began to take on a definite shape—one that had changed much from the original.

I had just taken up woodworking, so it was only natural for me to design and build our own Advent calendar. Ours would be different, of course, from the one we read about in Guideposts. Rather than being made out of paper or card stock, it would be a wooden box. Instead of little flaps, our calendar would have little doors with small compartments behind each one that hid a card, a tree ornament, or some other item that would help us tell a part of the real Christmas story every day. Being able to decide what was behind each door would give us greater flexibility than anything we could buy, and we could include things we felt were important that a card publisher might not consider profitable.

So, the concept of our Advent box came into being. Executing that idea became a real labor of love—heavy on the labor! First, I had to deal with the design questions. How tall, wide, and deep should it be? How do we make the compartments, and what size should they be? What do we use for door hinges and latches? What kind of finish do we put on it? Then came the actual work, which was not easy with my very limited supply of tools, skill, and experience! Cutting twenty–eight doors of the same size without a table saw or a radial arm saw was tedious and slow. Mounting those doors required one hinge per door with four screws, and a latch with two screws—all of which are very small and easily lost! With lots of love, however, the box was finished and has served us very

THE ADVENT BOX SITS IN OUR DINING ROOM

well over the years. Like our Advent wreath, the Advent box has stayed in good shape and will probably be an heirloom some day.

We made the actual Advent box 22.5" wide, 17.25" tall, and 7.25" deep from fir and pine, and finished the exterior with a walnut stain and three coats of polyurethane varnish. I made the hinges by cutting piano hinges into individual pieces with a hacksaw; this was inexpensive, but took a lot of work. I made the latches from two screws and an S–hook. Years later, when John was grown and married, I made a box for him and Missy, who is the finest daughter–in–law in the world. A quarter of a century of experience with woodworking projects and a better collection of tools made the job much easier. This time, though, I used oak instead of soft wood, which made a more beautiful box in most ways...but the original is still the best!

Now we had our box, but it was empty. All of its twenty–eight little doors opened smoothly and easily to reveal twenty–eight little compartments. In 1979, Christmas was on a Monday, so we had an Advent season of three weeks and one day—the shortest possible Advent season. But that still meant twenty–two Advent devotions to prepare for twenty–two little doors begging to reveal a wonderful truth about the Nativity of our Lord when opened by a not–quite–two–year–old boy. This was a challenge entirely different from designing and making the box, and it also turned into a labor of love of daunting proportions.

I began by listing all the Scriptures I could think of or find that had to do with the coming of Christ. You may think it's easy, and I did when I first started. But when I began to sort through my list for twenty–two different texts, each with a message all its own, then try to think of and make or find some object to illustrate that message, the task grew at an alarming rate and threatened to overwhelm the season! Although we only found a few objects to buy (with Judy making many more), or sometimes just put a picture in the box, we managed that first year.

Here are a few of our devotions from that first year, with their Bible text and object:

Isaiah 28:16: "So this is what the Sovereign LORD says: "See, I lay a stone in Zion, a tested stone, a precious cornerstone for a sure foundation; the one who trusts will never be dismayed." (NIV) Use a rock or piece of brick: just as our house is made of brick, so Jesus is the foundation of a good life.

Isaiah 51:11: "Therefore the redeemed of the LORD shall return, and come with singing unto Zion; and everlasting joy shall be upon their head: they shall obtain gladness and joy; and sorrow and mourning shall flee away." (KJV) We knew a fun song using the words of this verse, so we sang it several times. John couldn't sing with us, of course, but he was interested for a while!

Jeremiah 33:15: "In those days and at that time I will make a righteous Branch sprout from David's line; he will do what is just and right in the land." (NIV) We used a twig from a tree and said, "We sometimes talk about a family tree, with each of us being a branch. Jesus was the promised Righteous Branch of the family of King David."

I Thessalonians 4:16, 17: "For the Lord himself will come down from heaven, with a loud command, with the voice of the archangel and with the trumpet call of God, and the dead in Christ will rise first. After that, we who are still alive and are left will be caught up together with them in the clouds to meet the Lord in the air. And so we will be with the Lord forever." (NIV) We found a little trumpet tree ornament and put it in the box for this devotion on the Second Advent of Jesus.

Although these items were pretty simple, John, who was not yet two years old, probably did not grasp much of what was going on. Yet, he did love putting the trumpet on the tree, and after a few days he obviously looked forward to seeing what was in the box. That first year involved a great deal of work, and not a crowning success in some ways...then again, it was! For us, the season was not just one long prelude to opening a pile of gifts on Christmas Eve, nor was it a breathless, anxious wait to see what Santa Claus would bring to good little girls and boys. The Advent season was full of little truths (that are really never little) about Jesus and His coming to earth for us: a little baby in a manger became our King!

More than that, the first year was the beginning of a tradition. The next year, we as a family were looking forward to the season of Advent. The following year, it became part of who we were as a family: it was "how we do Christmas." Every year our devotions changed and generally improved. We kept some favorites and let others go that didn't go over very well or were no longer fitting for the ages and stages of our family.

Somewhere during the years of preparing, doing, learning, laughing, and playing, we found in the box the power to transform the whole Christmas season—to actually center it on Jesus Christ. That power came from the devotions themselves as they changed and grew over the years, with the addition of some important new, simple—but amazing—elements.

In Rebekah's Words

It's not just the neighbors' opinion of us. Good grief, sometimes *I* think we're crazy during Advent, but I wouldn't stop celebrating it for the world.

Of the three of us children, I've observed the fewest Advents (since I'm the baby), but I also had the advantage of coming along when everybody knew what kind of worked and what didn't. I probably have a stronger sense of tradition for some stuff, because I can't remember when we didn't do some of the same things every year.

Of course, being the youngest has other benefits, even though I can't believe I'm admitting it. When John and Joy Lin were married or away at college, I was just getting old enough to enjoy some of the things we did. Some of my favorite memories of Advent involve trekking out to the wilds of Oklahoma with Dad—and sometimes Mom—to find and cut down a Christmas tree for us. I don't remember why John and Joy Lin didn't go with us, but I know that I loved going out to help Dad pick out the tree. That was exciting! Another of my favorite memories is reading *Mickey's Christmas Carol*—and the real *Christmas Carol* by Charles Dickens—every year. For as long as I can remember, Dad and I have read the official, non–Disney version every year. I'm sure that's one of our Christmas activities I'll really miss at college this winter.

I realize that from what I've said so far it sounds like Dad was the only one who was really involved, but that certainly isn't true. Mom helped a lot, too. Unfortunately, my clearest memory of her contribution is negative....

It was during my junior year. I had just received the results of my PSAT, the test that qualifies students for a National Merit Scholarship. My score was good enough to qualify, so we were all very excited, of course. Now, we have a tradition of having a celebratory dinner when a member of our family does something exceptional, so we just assumed I would have mine that night. Unfortunately, Mom had control of the box that night and had already planned to eat outside, "like the shepherds." So, we ate steaks outside in the darkness and cold weather really quickly, because I had to work at the band concession stand at a basketball game that night.

I will never let my family forget that night.

Despite that one gripe (and a few others), my Advent memories are wonderful. And even that night served a purpose: I respect the shepherds more now, because they had to do that every night! Honestly, I have no idea what Christmas would be like without the box. From the bell in the first door to the gift and car in the last two, the box has really developed my conception of Christmas and always reminded me of the real "reason for the season."

Chapter Four

We Find Power in the Box

Our little tradition of having an object and a Bible verse in the box every time got a little boring sometime in the second year. Judy would have the meal ready, we would put John in his booster chair, and I would put all the excitement I could into seeing "what is in the box!" After a while, though, the little fellow in the booster chair was not so impressed, and I began to feel self–conscious, even if our audience was not quite three years old! So we introduced a change. When something went over well, we made another change, and then others over the years until we really had some excitement every time we opened the box, because we never knew what would be there.

The first innovation was this: Judy found a little imaginative story in *Virtue* magazine, and we just tore it out, folded it up, and put it in the box for that day. "Caleb the Camel," by Jean Holmes and illustrated by Chuck Reasoner, was a story that was just right for our pre–schooler. This "pretend" story, told in verse form, was about one of the camels the Wise Men may have ridden to Bethlehem. "Caleb the Camel" wasn't very long, and John loved it, so we read it over and over again. (You can read this story in one of the devotionals for the second week of Advent on page 64.)

Caleb found his way into the box again for many years after that, until we no longer had a pre–schooler with whom to share it. Two years after Caleb appeared, we had one "story night" for each week of Advent, so Caleb had company. The first to join him was "Martin the Cobbler," (as we called it), a *Reader's Digest* abridgement of Tolstoy's folktale "Where Love Is, God Is." This is a classic story of a pious cobbler in Russia who wondered whether he would welcome Jesus with love, or reject Him, as Simon, the wealthy Pharisee of Luke 7:36–50, had done. Although this tale written by a master storyteller is suitable for reading to small children, it has spiritual truths for all of our family to ponder, so we still read it regularly.

Also joining Caleb that year was one of our most valuable children's books, *Santa, Are You For Real?* by Harold Myra and joyfully illustrated by Dwight Walles. John, then almost four–years–old, was being exposed to Santa Claus, so we had to deal with Santa in some way. We knew that we did not want to get him started "believing" in Santa because we just did not believe telling our son a lie was right, no matter how "innocent" it might be or how popular. Neither did we want to be rigid and forbid all contact, making John some kind of pre–school censor for his friends; there is, after all, a lot of fun in Santa Claus!

Fortunately, Harold Myra, the president and CEO of Christianity Today International, felt the same way we did. He researched the subject and crafted a beautiful children's story that dealt delightfully, truthfully, and tactfully with this important issue. This enjoyable book opens with a small boy listening to the jeers of older children who no longer believe in Santa. To comfort him, his dad tells him the story of the real St. Nicholas, and the boy joyfully responds by "acting like St. Nick." Was it a success for us? After reading this delightful story, we never had any problem with Santa because our children did not experience the trauma of discovering that Santa is not real. Twenty–six–year–old John recently called this book, "My favoritest book ever!"

Our fourth story that year may raise some eyebrows among our readers. We read the children's illustrated version of the classic, "The Night Before Christmas" by Clement Moore. Yes, we read *the* poem that popularized Santa Claus with his reindeer, sleigh, and bag full of toys! We did not read it as a true story but as "pretend," which is perfectly acceptable for young children. Since we had already learned the story of the real St. Nicholas and how he passed into myth to become Santa, we were no longer afraid that John would get the wrong idea. As Judy said, we did not want our children to feel they missed out on something good because we had a Christ–centered Christmas. So, we read the book and had some fun—without believing in Santa. We found a little tree ornament of a slice of cheese with a mouse on it to put in the box, and for many years we all knew that finding it in the box meant we would read the altogether–pretend children's classic about the jolly old elf!

Appendices One and Two have lists with brief descriptions of the stories and books we have used as part of our Advent box adventure. Although we still read some of those stories and books every year, some were much more interesting to Dad than anyone else and lasted only one year. I am not sorry that we included them for one year, though, for they provided another important message during the Christmas season. Stories of POWs in Vietnam celebrating Christmas or World War II soldiers going home on a hospital ship at Christmas remind us that there are more serious aspects of Christmas than the newest toy or gadget! As technology improved, we added videos and DVD's to our book collection, including our favorite Christmas film, *It's a Wonderful Life*.

In those early years, as we were discovering stories and books to enrich the Christmas season, we also added devotions along with special activities to what we might find in the box. These were activities we would do together because they were based on the Advent of Jesus. A miniature Christmas tree that would just barely fit in our box, and the devotional that went along with it meant that we would decorate the Christmas tree that night. Some porcelain carol singers in another compartment indicated that our family would sing Christmas carols together that night; over the years, sometimes it meant we would go caroling in the neighborhood. Then there was the little blue Hot Wheels car which told our family that we were going "home to Grandma and Grandpa's" for Christmas, an activity that caused great rejoicing every year. Other major activities to go along with the devotions—located in part two of this book—included going Christmas shopping, sharing a silent meal, baking breads or candies for ourselves and others, eating a meal outside around a campfire (no matter what the weather may be), and, our all–time favorite—making gingerbread houses.

Now in addition to simple devotions with an object and a Bible verse, we have talked about using stories, books, and videos as part of the devotions and about including special activities. With this kind of variety, there is always some excitement about what might be found in the box! But there is still one other type of devotion to describe, one that really completes the transformation we were looking for to unleash the full power of the box. This is most easily introduced by describing the method I use to prepare for the first Sunday in Advent.

I begin by looking at a calendar sometime in the fall. On a yellow legal pad, I mark off four rows and seven columns with little squares. Then I insert the dates in an upper corner and write in the names and themes of the weeks on the Sundays. Events of the season come next: When is Christmas Eve? What about Hanukkah, St. Nicholas' Day, the Winter Solstice, and Pearl Harbor Day? What are the dates of the Christmas program at church, the band concert, the last day of school, and any parties and other events we know we must attend? I write all these important dates down to form the framework I'll work and build around. If we are not required to take part in some of these events, we sometimes choose early in the process not to participate, just to relieve the hectic pressure of the season. Advent is going to be very full, so we simplify wherever we can!

Placing these events on the calendar both opens possibilities and also reveals our constraints concerning devotions to go with the box. Possibilities abound for creative devotions that spring from these already scheduled events! We have often done special devotions in honor of Hanukkah. Pearl Harbor Day is an excellent time to do a devotion about Jesus being the Prince of Peace or the importance of praying for our leaders and the military. We also remind ourselves that Herod's attack upon the baby Jesus was even more infamous than the attack upon Pearl Harbor. Often on St. Nicholas' Day, we go over the origin of—and what is good about—Santa Claus.

The calendar also reveals our limitations—realities we dare not ignore. It tells us when we cannot do some things. One year, for instance, I had planned a nice quiet time of prayer for several groups of people with simple jobs, like the shepherds in the Christmas story, or our garbage collectors or janitors at the school; however, I had not put an event on the calendar, and we had only time for a quick prayer of blessing while seventeen–year–old Rebekah stood there with her car keys in hand, waiting to dash off to some commitment. Having our calendar in hand helps us avoid things like that.

When I have put the basic structure of the calendar together—and that really takes very little time—I start filling in the spaces with other activities we know we will do. When will we decorate the tree or the outside of the house? I write them down. Other things for the calendar might include Christmas shopping trips, going to Grandma and Grandpa's house, caroling, or baking cookies or breads to give as gifts. Get all these events on the calendar.

Here is the real capstone of the power of the box: find the spiritual significance for the events you have just put on your calendar. There should be a reason that we as Christians participate in these activities—or we shouldn't do them at all! If Jesus is Lord, a certain event must either be part of His will for us, or we should avoid it.

We find that special significance of an event and talk about it during our devotion for the day. For instance, why do we put lights on the outside of our house? It is not just because "everyone in the neighborhood does this, and our family always has." There is a reason that Christians do this. (See page 48 for our answer.) Again, why are we decorating a tree? What is the origin of that tradition, and why would we as Christians want to do it? (See page 51.) Why are we going shopping? Why do we give gifts at Christmas? What should our gifts say to the recipient? They ought to say more than, "Well, I have to get something for this person or I'll look bad." (See page 62.)

Now you can see the potential power of the box. When we search our hearts, minds, history, and the Scriptures for the meanings behind these events and then present these as the reasons for doing them, the Christmas season begins to revolve around Jesus and His work in history. Many common—sometimes tyrannical and demanding—parts of the season are put in their proper places; we do them because we want to show, proclaim, and experience the love of God in Jesus Christ! By doing this, we have created the means to put the spiritual significance of ordinary events in their proper place as the very reason we do them.

The power of the Advent box comes from the way it centers our lives on Jesus for that all–important season leading up to Christmas. After filling in our calendar with the events, activities, stories, books, Scriptures, and movies, our family has a daily exposure to some relevant truth or application from Scripture.

These activities are loosely arranged according to the meanings of the four weeks of Advent: plan, prepare, share, and rejoice. We participate in the same Christmas traditions other families do, read many of the same stories and watch some of the same movies, but we don't do them just because they are fun or traditional, although they are. We do them because they make Jesus known and bring our family closer together.

These elements turn our season into an experience with Jesus Christ. It's true that He has come as a baby in a manger, but He also gave his life so we can live! We must invite Him into our hearts, learn to live out His commands in our lives, and live in constant anticipation of His return to the earth to bring justice and love to their fullness. Day by day, through Scripture verses, stories, movies, and special activities, our Advent season centers on God's gift of Jesus Christ. We are not trying to make a place for Jesus in the hubbub of the modern American Christmas; we really are celebrating the coming of Jesus Christ. That transformation of Christmas is the actual power of the box!

That transformation was what we were looking for when we began using the Advent box. Before that was our quest for traditions to bind our family together. That happened as well; as Joy Lin says in her essay, "What the box means to me is FAMILY!" Again, we did not want to let our devotions become a tiresome burden, but rather wanted them to be fun. That goal was met beyond our wildest dreams, sometimes with just having warm hearts, and other times laughing together so hard that the tears came! We didn't want the Christmas season to be just one great, long, breathless sprint to the gifts under the tree; instead, for us, it has become a daily experience of anticipation—"What is in the box, and what adventure will we have today?"

One thing that happened, which we didn't really expect, was the spiritual growth that resulted from using the box. Of course, you will say, that is the whole reason to have family devotions—whether during Advent or any other time—and you are quite right. But, somehow, it took us by surprise as the years went along. There was the spiritual growth in Judy and me; undoubtedly, we understand the Christmas story more deeply than we ever thought possible. During the years, the growth of our children was heartening, as they understood the deeper meaning of the shepherds, Zechariah, or sharing with others. But we never anticipated the spiritual growth Missy speaks of when she and John began to put together their own devotions for their box! There is power in that box!

But does the box itself have anything to do with it? Couldn't you reach the same ends with some other method? I've thought many times that a simple cardboard box or even a paper sack, decorated and filled daily, could do the same thing in many ways. But there is something special about the box, sitting there in a prominent place, waiting for Advent to begin, raising curiosity about what adventures we will have this year. Then it sits there, in full view of curious little eyes, with one door open, then two, and on up to all seven for the first week, and so forth during the second and third weeks, and the last few days of the season found in the fourth week. In many ways it overshadows the Christmas tree and its gifts as the focal point of the season, drawing us closer, little door by little door, toward the advent of the Christ!

Finally, though, it is the devotions coming from those items we find in the box that carry the meaning and build the Advent season day by day. Perhaps you have thought while reading this section, "How do they do that?" I know that I've found it very difficult to keep from telling you more than you want to know, but I didn't want the narrative part of this book to get too long. So, Part Two is now ahead of us—as Judy says, "the fun part of the book"—the devotions themselves! Enjoy!

In Missy's Words, from Michigan

My experiences with the Advent box are limited compared to the rest of the family. I was "married into" the tradition of the box about five and a half years ago, and John and I received a box for Christmas two years ago. For the first year we had the box, we didn't "have time" to mess with it (we should have made time, but it didn't seem important), but we did use it this year. This year John and I experienced an adventure: we moved from Prague, Oklahoma, to Traverse City, Michigan—a long way from home! I grew up in the country, south of Paden about seven miles from Prague, so all my family and friends are in the Paden/Prague area; here in Traverse City we know very few people. So, far from home, we decided to do the box ourselves.

I was not working, so I took charge of it and did the devotions every day except Wednesdays and Saturdays, when John did them. At first I tried to think back to what we did when we went to Ben and Judy's for supper/lunch, but I wasn't having much luck remembering. So I called my wonderful mother–in–law for help and she told me about the weeks' meanings again and some of the things they've done. She gave me some good ideas, but not too many, since she wanted me to search for some on my own.

The first week (prophecy/planning) was hardest; I had to do a lot of research and asked plenty of questions, but finally decided I liked the first week best. Prophecy was cool! After looking in the dictionary, I searched the Bible and the Internet. There are tons of times in the Bible when something was prophesied in the Old Testament and then fulfilled in the New Testament! Wow, you should do a search for that!

During that first week, the Mennonite family we were renting from came to our home and ate supper with us. We introduced them to Advent and what it means to us. In the box that night was this:

What Are Your Plans?

Isaiah 7:14: "Therefore the Lord himself will give you a sign: The virgin will be with child and will give birth to a son, and will call him Immanuel." (NIV)

Matthew 1:22–23: "All this took place to fulfill what the Lord had said through the prophet: 'The virgin will be with child and will give birth to a son, and they will call him 'Immanuel'—which means, 'God with us.'" (NIV)

God planned the birth of Jesus, which was a very important plan for us! He probably thought long and hard about how to save His people. Let's talk about some of your plans. What are some plans you have made and/or will make in the future? What factors went into the planning? Prayer, consultation, meditation, and more prayer?

It was neat to look back and share some things we've prayed about, planned and seen fulfilled—from small plans to big plans. John and I had prayed about his job and moving away, and we ended up moving over a thousand miles away: that's big! I had prayed about when to invite our neighbors down to have supper with us: that event wasn't so big, but we had a great time. We also got to hear about the husband and wife's planning and the three boys' (ages sixteen to twenty-one) plans for the future, so we got to know them better through that.

This also goes to show you that the box isn't just for married people with children. John and I have no children but have had a good time with the box. This activity made us rack our brains and do research in the Bible and other places, as well as do things together even if it was only for a few minutes at a time. The box can help draw people together, so don't be afraid to share it with other family and friends.

PART TWO

The Devotions

Introduction

The following devotions are arranged roughly according to the weeks and themes of the Advent season, but you are certainly free to move them around at your discretion. This is especially true of the devotions we have prepared for certain events. For instance, the devotion for Pearl Harbor Day is included in the second week here, but December 7 sometimes falls on the first week. The devotion for the first day of Hanukkah is included in the fourth week, but the date of the holiday varies greatly on our calendar. Yet, it is always on the same day according to the Jewish calendar. Again, you might want to put your tree up during the second or third week, rather than the first week as we have scheduled it here, or you might not want to do a tree at all!

Each of the devotions has a Scripture text listed, but this does not mean that you must read that text out loud during the devotion. You may, if you desire, because reading Scriptures helps to establish the importance and authority of the Bible in the minds of children. What is most important here is that the one giving the devotion be familiar with the text and use it in some way—either by reading it, telling the story presented in the verses, or simply being aware that it is there. You must let your family know that the devotion is not just your clever creation!

We have included a few devotions that introduce certain stories or videos, though Appendices One and Two provide a more extensive list of stories and books we have used. In the following chapters, we include those that have had a special meaning to us over the years and show you how you might introduce them to your family. If you don't have access to these stories or books in your local library, area bookstores, or online...don't use them! Use some you like and can find instead.

Flexibility is essential, and creativity is the key to developing your own wonderful Advent traditions. It is our prayer that these devotions will bless you. We believe they can be used "right out of the book," but they are also intended to spark your own creativity. Use them, change them, and share them.

At the beginning of each chapter, we have included a special devotion for the Sundays, when the new candle of the week will be lit for the first time. On the first Sunday, you light the first candle, then light it again during your meal and devotion times for the rest of the week. On the second Sunday, a second candle is lit along with the first to burn throughout the week during your devotions and meals together. This pattern is continued throughout the four weeks of Advent. We have also included a special Christmas Eve devotion at the end of the fourth week for lighting the Christ candle. Like all the devotions, these are optional; use them if you like, make your own, or just light the candle! If you're getting a late start this year, you might just use these, without the daily devotions or an Advent box, just a wreath.

Our main desire is to make Jesus known in these devotions and to help you enjoy a Christ—centered Christmas season that brings your family together. May God the Creator, who has gifted you with creativity, bless you in your celebration of Christmas out of the Advent box.

In John's Words

Since the beginning of time (for me), the box has ushered in the Christmas season. What started out as a way to keep Christ in Christmas has evolved into so much more. I can remember the (mostly) friendly fights to see which of us kids would get to open the box each night. That excitement and suspense are still there, but now it is also a chance to settle down each day, take a deep breath, and detach from the frenzied days of the Christmas season. It is a chance to refocus and put things back into perspective.

Over time, we kids noticed a pattern for the items showing up in the box. The bell was always behind the first door. For years, Mom hung it inside a red wreath on the front door after lunch that day. (I can still hear that bell banging against the front door.) Dad has a favorite old shepherd made out of cotton and Styrofoam—a somewhat rough–looking fellow now who has had a rough life. That shepherd usually appeared in the box on Sunday of the Shepherds' week. A bag of dirty laundry, rolled up *Reader's Digest* stories, a plastic Christmas tree, a light bulb...all familiar tokens to us.

When we started getting older, Mom began to play a larger role in deciding what went into the box each day. Her creative mind was a bit different from Dad's. With Dad, it was normally doing something or reading something...with Mom it was usually eating something! It was her idea to put graham crackers in the box the first day of Bethlehem week, since Bethlehem means "House of Bread"...and what better way to ponder the mysteries of Bethlehem than by making Gingerbread Houses? During the Shepherds' week one year we made a little campfire outside and ate there, rather than inside (even though it was quite cool that evening). Mom figured that the shepherds didn't get to eat inside much...but I am fairly certain we ate much better than most shepherds (steak and baked potatoes, if I remember correctly).

My favorites have evolved over the years. When I was a kid, I always wanted to put up the Christmas lights or decorate the tree. As I've gotten older those activities are still fun, but they are only small parts of the real meaning of Christmas. One of my favorite things that show up in the box is a Santa Claus ornament, signaling that we will read *Santa, Are You for Real?*, a little book reminding us that the Santa Claus figure is derived from St. Nicholas, who spent his life serving Christ. Of course, the gift–wrapped piece of wood in the box on Christmas Eve is always fun...but even that has changed. Now it is more fun because we are getting to give the gifts.

The funny thing about getting older is that memories mean more to me. That old box has seen a lot of history and could tell a lot of stories. A few years back Dad made my wife and me our own Advent box...a nice, solid oak box to match some of our other furniture. It is undoubtedly prettier than the pine one that Dad has, but it doesn't hold the memories of the box that has watched over our weekday suppers and Sunday lunches for almost thirty Christmases now.

As the little Santa book says, in the closing words between the boy and his dad,

> *"The stories of reindeer, of snowflakes, and elves*
> *are holiday magic, when we think past ourselves."*
> *"I'll act like St. Nick," Todd said to his dad,*
> *"It's Jesus he loved—He makes us all glad!" (page 30)*

Chapter One

The First Week:
Prophecy and Planning

The first candle on the Advent wreath is called the Prophecy Candle, which signifies "planning." God planned for the advent of Christ long before His birth, and these plans were announced by the prophets. This can be a serious week of planning for the family, too—getting organized for Christmas. Some of the following devotions center on the prophecies of the first or second advents of Jesus; some concentrate on God's plans; and still others focus on our plans for the season or for life.

Lighting the Candle
Four Sundays before Christmas
The First Sunday in Advent: Prophecy/Planning
Read Isaiah 11:1–10

Centuries before Jesus was born in Bethlehem, God was planning for the great event of His birth. In the eighth century before Christ, Isaiah prophesied about the coming of the Christ to establish a kingdom of peace—eight hundred years before it happened!

God planned the place for Jesus' birth, the family or tribe from which He would come, and the effect of the birth. He arranged the time of His birth, and the place, time, and manner of His death. God has also destined that Jesus will return for a Second Advent. I have no doubt that God understands exactly when that will happen, though we do not. God made those plans and told us about them, at least in part, through the Hebrew prophets.

Do you think you can have the "perfect Christmas" without planning? No, Christmases that are memorable for their joy and spiritual depth don't just happen—so plan for them!

Use this week as a time of planning. Get out your calendar and fill it in. What are the major school dates to remember? What are the church events that need to be scheduled? When will you write and send your Christmas cards? By what date do you want to finish your shopping? When will you bake, put up the tree or have friends or family over for a meal? What parties are you expected to attend at work or in the community?

Got all that? Is your calendar full? Maybe you should be ruthless with an eraser! "No, we won't do that, or go there, or..." The perfect Christmas allows time to just enjoy the beauty of the season and each other, letting God give you surprises to enjoy and giving you an opportunity to bless people you know well or some you have never met.

Take time this week for planning. Better yet, do it today! Also, plan how you will keep Christ in Christmas this year. Light the Prophecy candle now, and light it during a family meal each day this week. It will help you center your life on Jesus during this Advent season.

What's in the Box? One silver bell

Every year since 1984 a small silver bell has been behind the first door of the box. It is our tradition, and we all look forward to it. Here are some of the devotional thoughts which have gone with the bell over the years:

• Exodus 28:35: Just as the bells on Aaron's robe rang when he entered the Holy Place, so we ring our bell to proclaim the beginning of Advent, a holy time of the year. This holy time proclaims: Joy! Peace! Love! Jesus has come, He is Lord, and He is coming again! We are going to celebrate Advent and Christmas because of Jesus our Lord.

- Revelation 22:7: The message of the Bible is as clear as a bell. Jesus came as a baby in a manger, which is why we celebrate Christmas. And just as clearly, the truth rings, "Receive Jesus as your personal Lord and Savior and be ready when He comes again."
- Luke 1:37 has the angel's last word to Mary: "For nothing is impossible with God." That message comes through at Christmas as clearly as a bell ringing. God became a man. A baby born in a manger is the King of the universe. This tiny babe is the Savior of the world. Nothing is impossible with God. Whatever God's will is for your life, it is possible!

What's in the Box? Christmas pencils for everyone

Scripture text: Proverbs 4:26 (TEV)

Special activity: Planning some things to do this Christmas

The point: This Scripture says, "Plan carefully what you do, and whatever you do will turn out right." Tonight we are going to do some planning for the Christmas season. We each have a pencil from the box so we can fill out this little family survey. When we're all finished, we'll discuss what is on them and make some plans. On each paper is:

Things we've done in the past at Christmas I'd like to do again:

   1.

   2.

   3.

New things I'd like to try this Christmas:

   1.

   2.

   3.

What's in the Box? A small cross

Scripture text: Isaiah 52:13—53:12

The point: Long before it happened, God had a plan for the birth of Jesus at Christmas and for His life, death, and resurrection. This text, written by the prophet Isaiah about eight hundred years before the birth of Christ, describes

God's plan for Jesus to carry the sins of the whole world in His body on the cross, and then to be raised from the dead and exalted to heaven. The cross is precious to us now because it was on a cross that Jesus died for sin, making it possible for us to be forgiven, receive the Holy Spirit, and have a place in heaven.

What's in the Box? **Anything that refers to Mr. Scrooge. For the children's version Judy made a little bag from scrap material and wrote, "Dirty Clothes" on it.**

Scripture text: Psalm 90:10–12

The point: In all our planning for our lives, we need to make sure we plan for eternity. In *A Christmas Carol* by Charles Dickens, Mr. Scrooge needed to do some planning for eternity. We are going to watch the video of the children's version of this story, *Mickey's Christmas Carol* (or begin reading the book itself, which will take more than one sitting). In the video you will see that Mr. Scrooge was so mean that he even made his little clerk do his laundry for almost no pay!

What's in the Box? **A bulb from a strand of outdoor Christmas lights**

Scripture text: Isaiah 9:2

Special activity: Decorating the outside of the house

The point: As Christians we talk about Jesus being the Light of the world because we have received Him as our Savior and realize that He helps us see things better. We can see and do what is right and pleasing to God because He lives in us. We want others to know this, so we put up lights at Christmas to tell the world that Jesus, the Light of the world, has come. So, tonight we are going to decorate the outside of the house with lights.

What's in the Box? **A magnifying glass**

Scripture text: Luke 1:46–56 (KJV or NRSV)

Special activity: Play with the magnifying glass. Children love this!

The point: Just as this magnifying glass makes things appear bigger than they are, Mary said, "My soul magnifies the Lord..." (verse 46) But she was not trying to make God bigger just to show people how big God really is, because so many think God is very small and not important at all. Mary wanted them to know that God was great and was doing great things in her life, so she sang this beautiful song. This song, called the Magnificat, is still sung in many churches today. He is still great and is doing great things in the lives of those who trust in Him.

What's in the Box? A small tree branch

Scripture text: Jeremiah 33:14–21

The point: Six hundred years before Jesus was born, God revealed His plan through the prophet Jeremiah for the Savior to come to earth as a descendant of King David. Just as we talk of a family tree, so He is called the Branch of David, the heir to his throne. With this distinctive prophecy, God reassures us that His promise of salvation could not be broken! Jesus is that Branch of David, the promised Messiah.

What's in the Box? A crossword puzzle

Down

1. None of His bones were _____.

New Testament	John 19:33
Old Testament	Psalm 34:20

2. He was given _____ when He was thirsty.

New Testament	John 19:29
Old Testament	Psalm 69:21

3. They cast _____ for His garments.

New Testament	Mark 15:24
Old Testament	Psalm 22:18

4. He was sold for 30 pieces of _____.

New Testament	Matthew 26:15
Old Testament	Zechariah 11:12

5. One of His characteristics was _____.

New Testament	Luke 2:52
Old Testament	Isaiah 11:2

Across

1. He was born in _____.

New Testament	Matthew 2:1
Old Testament	Micah 5:2

2. His mother was a _____.

New Testament	Luke 1: 26, 27
Old Testament	Isaiah 7:14

6. He rode into town on an _____.

New Testament	John 12:14
Old Testament	Zechariah 9:9

The point: Many prophecies about Jesus found in the Old Testament have been fulfilled in the New Testament.

Procedure: Divide your family into two teams. Give each a KJV Bible to use. Have one fill in the puzzle using the New Testament references and the other using the Old Testament references. Then compare the results!

What's in the Box? A star tree ornament

Scripture text: Matthew 2:1–11

Special activity: Star gazing

The point: The Magi saw the star and they followed it to Jesus. But how far in advance did God have to plan for that star to appear at just the right time and just the right place? Tonight we're going to go out and just look at the stars and think about how big they are and how far they are away from us, along with how God planned so long ago for that one special star. (If you live in a town or city, it will be helpful to go outside of town where the glare of the lights is less, so you can see the stars better. Many people in America have never really seen the stars in a dark night sky to experience the immensity of the universe; this could be a gift your children will long remember. These are the stars the shepherds saw every night and the ones that formed the background for the Star of Bethlehem.)

What's in the Box? Toy ax

(Open the door at breakfast, or announce that the tree will be cut "tomorrow after school.")

Scripture text: Psalm 96:11–13

Special activity: Select and cut down a Christmas tree. This will take some advance preparation, including finding out where to get it, the tools needed, any costs, and what kind of transportation will be needed for the cut tree.

The point: This text speaks of all the trees singing for joy before the Lord when Jesus comes again to make everything right. Won't that be a wonderful song to hear? Today we sometimes speak of the wind singing or whispering in the trees; we're just saying that, in their own way, they are praising the Lord. We have a tradition of bringing a tree into our home at Christmas, as part of our worship and praise of Jesus. We are going to go pick out, cut down, and bring home our tree today.

What's in the Box? A card upon which you have written something like, *"What was it like for Zechariah to be unable to speak a word? To help us find out, we will eat supper tonight in silence: there will be no talking! His silence was broken only by prayer after his son John was born; ours will be broken by prayer at the end of our meal."*

Scripture text: Luke 1:1–20

Special activity: Eat in silence.

The point: Tell the story of Zechariah not believing the angel's message, and read verse 20. You will all appreciate this experience of Zechariah more after this silent meal.

What's in the Box? A tiny mailbox or a new Christmas card

Scripture text: 3 John 13–14

Special activity: Sign and address Christmas cards. Even the youngest can make a mark, and the older children can help seal and stamp the envelopes.

The point: We would like to spend Christmas with all our friends and relatives who are special to us, but we can't because they live in many different places. So, just as the apostle John wrote to his friends when he could not be with them, we are going to send our greetings in Christmas cards to many of our friends. Tonight we are going to work together as a family to sign, address, seal, and stamp our Christmas cards that tell of Jesus' birth.

What's in the Box? A miniature Christmas tree

Scripture text: Psalm 121:1, 2; Isaiah 61:1

Special activity: Put up and decorate the Christmas tree.

The point: The origin of the Christmas tree is not clear. The practice of decorating a tree inside our homes in honor of Jesus originated in Germany, and legend has it that Martin Luther began the tradition. One crisp Christmas Eve, in the mid-1500s, he was walking through snow-covered woods and was struck by the beauty of a group of small evergreens. Their branches, sparkling from the snow reflecting the moonlight, reminded him of the stars over Bethlehem. When he got home, he set up a little fir tree indoors so he could share this story with his children. He decorated it with candles, which he lit in honor of Christ's birth.

Whatever its origin, the purpose of the Christmas tree originally was to glorify Jesus, and that is why we have one in our home. Tonight we will decorate our tree with lights because Jesus is the Light of the world, with ornaments that remind us of Him and what He has done, and with other adornments that are just pretty, because what God did at Christmas is beautiful.

What's in the Box? **A small dove figurine tree decoration**

Scripture text: Luke 1:39–45

The point: Before reading the Scripture text, ask the question, "In the Bible, the dove is often a symbol of the Holy Spirit. In the New Testament, who was the first one said to have been filled with the Holy Spirit?" Though the Holy Spirit was at work before this, and the Spirit "came upon and overshadowed" Mary, it was Elizabeth, the mother of John the Baptist, who was the first person in the New Testament to be filled with the Holy Spirit. Now, of course, because of the finished work of Jesus, all believers in Jesus can be filled with the Spirit.

Chapter Two

THE SECOND WEEK:
Bethlehem and Preparation

The second candle on the Advent wreath is called the Bethlehem candle, with its special meaning being "Preparation." Just as God prepared for the registration of the descendants from the tribe of Judah at Bethlehem, along with many other details surrounding the birth of Jesus, so we also have much preparation to do for Christmas.

Lighting the Candle
Three Sundays before Christmas
The Second Sunday in Advent: Bethlehem/Preparation
Read Micah 5:2–4

God made His plans, but as we know, the best intentions and plans come to nothing without good preparation and follow–through. So, God prepared for the birth of Jesus in Bethlehem. Have you ever thought about how much preparation it took to make sure that Mary got from Nazareth to Bethlehem for the birth? Or how much preparation it took to ensure the appearance of the star—however it was done and whatever it was—on the very night of Christ's birth? Yes, God planned, and then he prepared for the birth of Jesus in Bethlehem.

Likewise, we need to prepare for the fullest and least stressful celebration of Christmas possible. Are you going to bake cookies on Saturday? Make sure you have all of the ingredients. Are you going to put up the lights? Buy extra bulbs, because some of them may be burned out. Are you going shopping? Be prepared by knowing what you're looking for and what your budget will allow.

Where is Christ in all of this? Are you preparing your heart to receive Jesus Christ anew? This is very much what Advent is all about. Yes, Jesus came, and He is coming again. But right now, Jesus lives in our hearts through the Holy Spirit. Prepare to welcome Him once again.

Prepare this week, not only for celebrating the coming of Christ, but for Christ to come into your heart and family again. Light the Bethlehem candle now, remembering how God prepared for Jesus' birth in Bethlehem.

What's in the Box? A gingerbread house tree ornament

Scripture text: Ruth 1:22; Matthew 2:1–6

Special activity: Making gingerbread houses

The point: Bethlehem, where Jesus was born, was a small town about six miles south of Jerusalem. Its history in Israel was rich as the setting for the Book of Ruth and the hometown of King David. Bethlehem means, "City of Bread," though no one knows how that name came into being; probably at one time, the town was famous for its bread.

Over the centuries, people laughed a lot and did many fun things in Bethlehem. Think about David and his seven brothers or Jesus and his brothers and sisters; I'm sure they all laughed and had loads of fun there in Bethlehem. We will do something fun today: making gingerbread houses! These are often associated with Christmas, especially in Germany where some cities are famous for their gingerbread and the wonderful gingerbread houses decorated there at Christmas. We are going to make pretty simple houses using graham crackers, which will be provided. But each of you must go to the store and get some ingredient(s) that we can use to decorate the houses. Then we will gather back here to have a fun time making our own gingerbread houses!

The Basic Gingerbread House

1 large paper plate, white or colored, on which to build each house
6–7 full-sized graham crackers for each standard house
1 package almond bark, melted and kept warm in a crock pot
1 recipe Butter Cream cake frosting (below) OR Royal cake icing
found in some department stores or cake decorating supply stores
Cake decorating bags and tips (optional, to provide possibilities
for decorating)

Butter Cream Icing Recipe:

1¼ cups Crisco shortening
½ cup water
1 teaspoon vanilla extract
Pinch salt
2 pounds powdered sugar

Combine and beat at medium speed for approximately 10 minutes
(using a heavy-duty stand mixer). If you're using a hand mixer, it is
best to cut the recipe in half. Store in an airtight container.

House decorations, such as the following (but use your imagination!):
Stick pretzels, for windows, doors, fences, trees, etc.
Coconut flakes for snow
Cereals (Raisin Bran works well for roof shingles, using either raisins
or flakes)
Peanuts make nice rocks for walls or walks
Mini M&Ms, Tic-Tacs, or gumdrops for lights
Sprinkles
Mini-marshmallows make nice snowmen
Lifesavers

Directions: Each house requires six or seven full-sized graham
crackers, including three for the walls, two for the roof, one to shape
the gable ends of the roof, and one for the floor. The floor isn't
necessary, but it does make it easier to keep the walls square. If you do
use a floor, carefully cut away about ¼ inch from the narrow end, so
the walls will fit right.

Either dip the edges of the crackers, one at a time, in the melted bark or use a spoon to drizzle some on the edge. Then gently hold the pieces in place until the bark begins to cool and the structure holds together. This takes practice and patience.

Carefully, using a fairly sharp knife, cut two half–pieces of a cracker into the isosceles triangles needed for the roof (Dad often gets conned into doing this part for several family members). Coat the bottom edges with bark and hold in place until they stay, then drizzle bark on the upper edges and put the roof pieces in place.

When the walls and roof are firm, put more bark coating or cake frosting on the seams to make the structure stronger.

That is the basic structure! Now, turn your inner child loose and, using the decorating ingredients, create your masterpiece!

Note: You can make your houses as simple or extravagant as you want. The important thing to remember is that they don't have to be perfect; the objective is to have fun as a family. You must plan and prepare for all of this ahead of time. You may want to have all the ingredients on hand, rather than having family members provide some, depending on the ages of your children and other factors. We do this on Sunday afternoon, when we have several hours free—and we have no doubt that this is much more important than any football game on TV.

GINGERBREAD HOUSES ON DISPLAY—FUN, BUT NOT MASTERPIECES.

What's in the Box? A star

Scripture text: Matthew 2:1, 2, 9, 10

The point: The three wise men were part of an ancient tradition of scholar–priest–government officials from some Eastern land. No one is exactly sure from where they came, though many believe it was Persia; what we do know is that they belonged to this educated class because their title was the "Magi." (Calling them "kings" is probably a stretch, though they were members of the ruling class.) A large part of their education involved their religion, which largely dealt with the study of the stars and the interpretation of their placement and apparent movement. So, when the God of the universe wanted to get a message to them, He showed them a supernatural phenomenon among the stars. They knew from their interpretation of this new star that the "king of the Jews" was born in Israel, and that star led them right to the house where Jesus was.

No one knows what this star was. Was it a planet? A group of planets? An asteroid? An exploding star? Or was it something entirely supernatural? Whatever the star was, we know that God prepared it in advance. Did He do it quite suddenly and supernaturally? Even then, there must have been much to do to get it together. Or did he take a thousand years or more to move a star into just the right position and cause it to explode at just the right time?

However God did it, the star tells us plainly that God made great preparation for the advent of Jesus. He has plans in place and is preparing for His coming again. He is also preparing a good future for you.

What's in the Box? Matches or a scruffy angel

Scripture text: I Samuel 16:7

Special activity: Begin reading *The Best Christmas Pageant Ever.*

The point: Many of us have this problem of judging people by their outward appearance, not considering that they are—just as we are—created in the image of God and able to become great in His kingdom. Just as Samuel didn't think the boy David was good king material, we sometimes don't think others will become good people at all. Then there is the problem of growing weary of the Christmas story; if we are part of the same Christmas pageant year after year, it can get dull. The story we are going to begin reading tonight is about just such a situation. A whole family, along with their church, had grown bored with the annual Christmas program. They also didn't think the Herdman children, who burned down a tool shed trying to light all the chemicals in a stolen chemistry set (the reason for the matches in the box), were right for their church. Then they showed up at Sunday school just in time to claim all the leading parts for the pageant. What everyone thought was sure to end up in disaster turned out to be *The Best Christmas Pageant Ever*!

What's in the Box? Santa tree ornament

Scripture text: Matthew 1:24, 25

Special event: December 6, Saint Nicholas Day

The point: We know that Christmas is the celebration of the birth of Jesus. His mother was Mary, and she was the wife of Joseph. They were visited by shepherds and the Wise Men. But where does Santa Claus come into all of this? We are going to read a little book tonight that answers this important question: *Santa, Are You for Real?* by Harold Myra. This is especially fitting, since this is Saint Nicholas Day, the date on the church calendar set aside long ago as a special day to remember this great Christian from the early centuries of the church.

What's in the Box? Heart tree ornament

Scripture text: Galatians 4:4–7

The point: After all the preparations, at the exact right time, God sent Jesus into the world to be born in Bethlehem, so we could become children of God. When we become children of God by placing our faith in the Lord Jesus Christ, He puts His Spirit into our hearts. We are hanging this little heart on the tree to remind us that we must ask Jesus into our hearts and always make Him feel welcome there.

What's in the Box? A tiny manger

Scripture text: Luke 2:4–7 or Micah 5:2

The point: God had been preparing a place for the birth of Jesus for a thousand years before it happened! A few miles from Jerusalem, this little town of Bethlehem in Judea was the hometown of David, the greatest king of Israel, who was born about one thousand years before Jesus. About seven hundred years before Jesus, the prophet Micah announced that the "One who will be ruler over Israel" would be born in Bethlehem.

So, if God had been preparing for this great event for a thousand years, why was Jesus born in a stable and laid in a manger, a feeding trough for horses or cattle? Why wasn't there a nice bed ready for Him? Wasn't this a lack of preparation on God's part? Not at all! Jesus' birth in a manger gave Him the humble beginning with which the poorest of the world's people would identify. It was not only a place where common shepherds could feel comfortable, but also one where the richest of the Magi would have to humble themselves.

This little manger reminds us that even when we don't think things have worked out just right, God has not been fooled! He has indeed prepared something good for us!

What's in the Box? **A scepter**

Scripture text: Genesis 49: 8–12

The point: In ancient times, and nowadays in many parts of the world, it was the first–born son who inherited the right to rule, but Judah was born fourth in line in Jacob's family of twelve sons. However, Jacob's first–born, Reuben, had sinned against him very badly! Then the second and third sons, Simeon and Levi, were declared unfit to rule because they took advantage of the weakness of a whole village and slaughtered all the men. Judah, although not without his faults, had shown himself to be worthy, because he pledged his life for the safety of his brother Benjamin.

In this text, Jacob blessed Judah with the right to rule the people of Israel. King David was from the tribe of Judah, so he could rule as king, according to this blessing. As a descendant of David, Jesus is the one in whom this promise is fulfilled. Jesus is called in this text "the one to whom the scepter (the symbol of kingly authority) belongs." He is worthy to rule the world, our family, and our lives.

What's in the Box? Recipe for cookies, candy, or bread

Scripture text: Nehemiah 8:10

Special activity: Bake special food to give away this Christmas season.

The point: The day spoken of in our text was one in which the people heard the Word of God, and their leader, Nehemiah, instructed them not to be sad but to celebrate, eating good food and sending some to others. That is part of how we celebrate the coming of the Word of God, Jesus, at Christmas too. This is Bethlehem week—the week of preparation. Tonight we are going to prepare some buttermilk cinnamon bread (or candy) to share with friends and neighbors later. Be thinking of those with whom you would like to share this bread!

Buttermilk Cinnamon Bread

(Makes eight 8"x 3.75"x 2.5" loaf pans)

12 cups all-purpose flour

6 teaspoons baking soda

3 teaspoons salt

1½ cups canola oil

6½ cups sugar, divided (put 4½ cups in dough and save 2 cups for middle and topping)

6 cups buttermilk

6 eggs

2½ tablespoons cinnamon

4 tablespoons finely chopped walnuts or pecans, for garnish

In a large mixing bowl, combine flour, baking soda, and salt. In a smaller bowl combine oil and sugar (4½ cups). Add buttermilk and eggs; mix well. Stir into dry ingredients just until moistened. Spray pans with cooking spray. Put 1 cup batter in each pan. Top with ⅛ cup cinnamon–sugar mixture. Put 1 more cup of batter on top of that. Sprinkle each with ⅛ cup more sugar–cinnamon mixture. Sprinkle with nuts. Bake at 350° for about 45 minutes. Cool; then wrap with clear wrap and decorate as desired. Loaves may be frozen for giving later.

Spiced Pecans

1 egg white, beaten slightly
½ teaspoon salt
1 tablespoon water
1 teaspoon cinnamon
3 cups pecan halves
½ teaspoon ground cloves
½ cup sugar
½ teaspoon ground nutmeg

In a small bowl, beat together the egg white and water. Stir in the pecans, stirring until all surfaces are moistened. Mix together the sugar, salt, cinnamon, cloves and nutmeg; sprinkle over pecans, mixing well. Spread pecans on a lightly greased or foil-lined cookie sheet and bake in pre–heated 300° oven for 20 minutes. Stir every 5 minutes to crisp and dry pecans evenly. Cool and store in baggies to give away—or eat!

What's in the Box? Tiny musical instrument

Scripture text: Luke 2:13, 14
Special activity: Attending a Christmas concert
The point: When the heavenly host was praising God at the birth of Jesus, they were doing it with music! Ever since then, people have been making music in praise of Jesus, and some of our greatest music is written for the Christmas season. Tonight we are going to attend a Christmas concert.

What's in the Box? New Christmas earrings for Mom

Scripture text: Proverbs 31:21
Special activity: Give each family member a new piece of Christmas clothing.
The point: (This is one of Judy's devotions.) "Oh, look! Cute earrings for me! One of the jobs of a wife and mother is making sure that everyone in the family has appropriate clothes to wear. During the Christmas season, we have lots of opportunities to wear fun 'Christmas' clothes that we can't wear the rest of the year. So, I've been doing some preparing and shopping myself this week.

Tonight, you each have a gift to open containing something you can enjoy wearing throughout the season. Hope you like your new clothes!"

What's in the Box? Bow for a present

Scripture text: John 3:16

The point: This bow needs to be on a gift! But I don't have a gift to put it on, so I had better go make one or buy one. Is that the only reason I should give a gift to someone, just so I can have something to put this bow on? No! The reason we give gifts at Christmas is to show our love for those to whom we give them. John 3:16 says, "For God so loved the world that He gave..." and that is why we give too. Christmas is a time every year when we give gifts to others, just to say, "I love you," just like God loved us and sent Jesus at that first Christmas.

So, to get ready for Christmas and the giving of these gifts of love, we are going shopping on (state the day). You will each need to prepare for the shopping trip by thinking and praying about each person to whom you will give a gift and making a list of what you hope to find, being careful to keep within your budget. You can either buy the gift or things you need to make it.

What's in the Box? A sword

Scripture text: Matthew 2:16–18

Special event: Pearl Harbor Day, December 7

The point: This part of the Christmas story is often left out, for it is neither beautiful nor fun. In fact, it is terrible. Herod was a ruthless king who was not above killing his own wife or son and did not hesitate, in this instance, to murder a large number of small, innocent boys just to eliminate a possible rival to his throne. We can only imagine the terror that swept the area, and the horrible grief of the families who had children that were killed in cold blood. We are eternally grateful that an angel warned Joseph of the danger and that he acted quickly, taking his family to Egypt until the danger was past.

The Bible includes this story because it is true. Life was not always pleasant or safe for Jesus, and it is the same for us. This is Pearl Harbor Day, a date of special importance for Americans. In a very successful surprise attack on this day in 1941, Imperial Japan bombed our naval base in Pearl Harbor, Hawaii, and plunged the United States into World War II. It is a day that President Franklin Roosevelt said, "will live in infamy!" We lost 2,280 troops and almost 1,100 were wounded, along with more than a dozen ships destroyed, including two battleships, and six other battleships were badly damaged. More than one hundred and fifty airplanes were destroyed, and the entire area suffered serious damage.

Herod's attack on innocent children and the Japanese attack on Pearl Harbor are not the only terrible things that have happened. The devil is very real, very evil, and inspires great wickedness in some men. But, this horrible massacre is included in the Christmas story that also proclaims the coming of the Prince of Peace, the Messiah! Evil has not won, nor will it in the end! Meanwhile, like Joseph, we can depend upon God for our protection and guidance. Evil will be able to slip in some vicious attacks, sometimes hitting us; but the fact that we celebrate Christmas is our testimony to the very real victory of Jesus over all the forces of darkness.

Free people have always needed those who would, under God, protect them from evil people, as our soldiers do today. Since many of our soldiers are a long way from home at this Christmas season in dangerous places and may feel very lonely, let's take some time now to pray for their safety and for God's presence with them.

What's in the Box? A trumpet tree ornament

Scripture text: 1 Thessalonians 4:14–18

The point: One day the trumpet of God will sound, announcing the second coming of Jesus, and we shall go to meet Him in the air! This "Second Advent" will bring about the fulfillment of all the prophecies of the Messiah that have not yet been completed, and it will be much different from His first Advent when He was born in Bethlehem. Then, very few people knew about His birth, but when He comes again, everyone will know! In Bethlehem, He came as a helpless baby; the second time, He will come as a great King, a conqueror who will rule the world with justice and power. So be prepared! Keep the love of Jesus in your heart and live for Him every day.

What's in the Box? A camel

Scripture text: Matthew 2:1

The point: Those wise men, or kings as they are often called, came a long way, no doubt riding camels. What was it like on that long journey? What was it like for them, and what was it like for their animals? Well, we are going to read a pretend story about how it may have been for one of the camels on that journey.

"Caleb the Camel" by Jean Holmes
(reprinted by permission of the publisher)

Many long years ago
in a faraway land, there lived a small camel called
Caleb the Grand.
Why such a name?
Why not Henry or Lyle?
Well…Caleb was grand because
of his smile.
His great under lip turned up at
each side, so he smiled
and he smiled
and he smiled
broad and wide.
Just why did he smile?
Well, nobody knew, but
he smiled
and he smiled
and he smiled
and he grew.
Caleb romped in the desert.
He played in the sand.
He followed his mother all about
the strange land.
His knees were so knobby…
He had a large bump…
His head was enormous…
His tail just a stump.
Not much to look at, no not much
at all,

Awkward, clumsy,
gawky, tall.
"So why is he smiling?"
Other camels would say,
"He smiles through the night
and he smiles through the day."
They tried to ignore him
"Push Caleb aside...if he comes
out to play we'll all run
and hide."
"If you smile one more time
we'll spit on you too."
Caleb smiled
and he smiled
and he smiled
and he grew.
His mother was sorry 'bout the way
he was treated.
Caleb never complained,
never cried, never bleated.
"I'm special you know,
I can feel it inside.
They may hurt my feelings...
they won't hurt my pride.
"I know that I'm different,
but I'm loved, I'm content."
Smiling all through the years...
Was that what it meant?
"My moment will come,
but when? But how?"
Caleb smiled, not knowing that his
moment was now.
For now...Right now
in the still of the night,
a star shone in the sky, glistening,
gleaming so bright...
That it lighted the desert
almost light as day,

it shone down on a caravan
not far away.
Miles and miles onward,
day after day.
The star led to a stable and
a babe in the hay.
Caleb watched as the caravan came
into sight…he saw camels and kings
and the star shining bright.
Oh yes, he was frightened,
scared through and through,
but he watched and he smiled and
he gulped a bit too.
The caravan stopped
and a young king called out,
"I need a fresh camel…
for mine has the gout."
"Will one of you take me on my
journey afar, to Bethlehem City,
I must follow the star."
All the camels leaped forward
each shouting, "Take me…"
"I'm handsome""Reliable"
"Strong as can be."
Caleb stood silently,
watched all the while.
"You there," said the king,
"You there, with the smile."
Caleb knelt as the king climbed onto
his hump.
Caleb raised up…then tripped—
and the king bounced
bump…bump.
Other camels laughed out,
"That Caleb can't do it."
Caleb's mother was pleased…
"Yes, you can, son. Hop to it."

Caleb held his head proud,
held his head high, and they
followed the star shining there
in the sky.
A babe, oh so tiny,
in this faraway town...
And shepherds and angels
and music all 'round.
"What's happening?" thought Caleb.
"What can this be? This babe
in the manger...
I've just got to see."
So he ever so carefully knelt down
near the child, the little Lord
Jesus, so tender and mild...
Reached out His small hand and He
touched Caleb's nose.
Caleb tingled with joy, clear down
to his toes.
Caleb felt special...
somehow set apart, there were
tears in his eyes but he smiled
with his heart.
The end of the story, well, Caleb grew
old, and all through the years
here's the story he told.
"Different? Who cares?
Just remember to smile,
the Lord touches us all
every once in a while."

Chapter Three

THE THIRD WEEK:
Shepherds and Sharing

The third candle on the Advent wreath is called the Shepherds' candle, with its special meaning of "Sharing." When the shepherds had seen the baby Jesus, the Bible says they went and shared what they had seen and heard with everyone. Christmas has been a time of sharing ever since. The devotions this week will focus on the shepherds, their sharing, and our sharing with others.

Lighting the Candle
Two Sundays before Christmas
The Third Sunday in Advent: Shepherds/Sharing
Read Luke 2:8–20

The shepherds "made known the saying that had been told them," the fact that this infant was, indeed, the long–awaited Messiah. They apparently shared this good news with all who would listen. So, the Shepherds' candle represents sharing.

God shared His Son with us, but it was much more than that. He gave Him to us—the world. God did not hold back on His gift, nor did he ask for Christ back. He gave us Jesus without reservation.

What can we share this week of Advent season? Of course, we will give gifts, but we all know that many of them are expected and we are just fulfilling our obligations, rather than sharing....unless we really put ourselves into these gifts and they actually become an expression of our love. So, think about each person and pray for him or her. Wrap each gift with paper and prayer. If you can, deliver gifts in person with a special word of love and appreciation.

What else can you share this week? A special phone call? A special card or letter? A special smile or visit? Do it!

Also, take the time to share with someone the real meaning of Christmas. Perhaps a co–worker or neighbor does not know Jesus Christ. You could begin with your simple testimony: "This is the Christmas season, and I would like to share with you why this is so important to me." Then share the fact that Jesus has made a big difference in your life. Tell the story of your personal encounter with Christ. It will be appreciated by your listener.

Light the Shepherds' candle now, being mindful of how God shared His love, how the shepherds shared the story of Christ's birth, and how you can share the gospel message with others this week.

What's in the Box? A shepherd figurine

Scripture text: Luke 2:8

Special activity: Eat outside, as the shepherds did (Open the box in the morning)

The point: Have you ever thought about what it would have been like to be a shepherd at the time of Jesus' birth? It was probably very boring watching a flock of sheep day in and day out. There were no fast–food places they could run to for a quick meal or a coke for a mid–afternoon picker–upper. They had to cook their food on–site and eat and sleep outside in all kinds of weather. That was a lot different from how we live now!

So, to get a little bit more of a "feel" for the shepherds in the Christmas story, tonight we are going to eat supper outside—no matter what the weather.

What's in the Box? Little baby figure cut out of felt

Special activity: Read "A Russian Christmas Story 'FOR ALWAYS'" by Will Fish

(Reprinted by permission of the publisher.)

In 1994, two Americans answered an invitation from the Russian Department of Education to teach morals and ethics (based on biblical principles) in the public schools. They were invited to teach at prisons, businesses, the fire and police departments, and a large orphanage. About 100 boys and girls who had been abandoned, abused, and left in the care of a government–run program were in the orphanage.

They related the following story in their own words. "It was nearing the holiday season, 1994, time for our orphans to hear—for the first time—the traditional story of Christmas. We told them about Mary and Joseph arriving in Bethlehem. Finding no room in the inn, the couple went to a stable, where the baby Jesus was born and placed in a manger. Throughout the story, the children and orphanage staff sat in amazement as they listened. Some sat on the edges of their stools, trying to grasp every word.

"Completing the story, we gave the children three small pieces of cardboard to make a crude manger. Each child was given a small paper square, cut from yellow napkins I had brought with me. No colored paper was available in the city. Following instructions, the children tore the paper and carefully laid strips in the manger for straw. Small squares of flannel, cut from a worn–out nightgown an American lady was throwing away as she left Russia, were used for the baby's blanket. A doll–like baby was cut from tan felt we had brought from the United States.

"The orphans were busy assembling their manger as I walked among them to see if they needed any help. All went well until I got to one table where little Misha sat—he looked to be about 6 years old and had finished his project. As I looked at the little boy's manger, I was startled to see not one, but two babies in the manger.

"Quickly, I called for the translator to ask the lad why there were two babies in the manger. Crossing his arms in front of him and looking at his completed manger scene, the child began to repeat the story very seriously. For such a young boy, who had only heard the Christmas story once, he related the happenings accurately—until he came to the part where Mary put the baby Jesus in the manger.

"Then Misha started to ad lib. He made up his own ending to the story as he said, 'And when Maria laid the baby in the manger, Jesus looked at me and asked me if I had a place to stay. I told him I have no mamma

and I have no papa, so I don't have any place to stay. Then Jesus told me I could stay with him. But I told him I couldn't, because I didn't have a gift to give him like everybody else did. But I wanted to stay with Jesus so much, so I thought about what I had that maybe I could use for a gift. I thought maybe if I kept him warm, that would be a good gift. So I asked Jesus, "Oh, if I keep you warm, will that be a good enough gift?" And Jesus told me, "If you keep me warm, that will be the best gift anybody ever gave me." So I got into the manger, and then Jesus looked at me and he told me I could stay with him—for always.'

"As little Misha finished his story, his eyes brimmed full of tears that splashed down his little cheeks. Putting his hand over his face, his head dropped to the table and his shoulders shook as he sobbed and sobbed. The little orphan had found someone who would never abandon nor abuse him, someone who would stay with him—FOR ALWAYS."

What's in the Box? Church tree ornament

Scripture text: Matthew 2:1, 2

Special activity: Go watch, or be a part of, a local church Christmas program.

The point: When the Wise Men knew the King of the Jews had been born, they got together and traveled a long distance to worship Him. Ever since then, people have traveled short and long distances just to worship Jesus together with others who love Him. Tonight our church has a special time of worship when the story of His birth is told again: our Christmas program. Tonight we are going to attend (or be a part of it) and worship as the Wise Men did.

What's in the Box? Perfume

Scripture text: Matthew 2:11

The point: The wise men brought Jesus three gifts which were common in that day—gold, frankincense, and myrrh. We use gold today for rings and jewelry, so we know what that is. Frankincense was a special type of incense; many people still burn incense today to make their place smell good or offer worship to God. Myrrh was fragrant oil extracted from the myrrh plant that is very common in southern Arabia. It was used as an important part of the beauty treatment given to Queen Esther (Esther 2:12) and was one of the perfumes used by "the Beloved" in the Song of Solomon (Song 3:6; 5:5). We might think it strange that myrrh was also used as part of the spices for embalming a dead body; Nicodemus brought it to the burial of Jesus (John 19:39).

No doubt the Wise Men brought myrrh because it was very valuable—a gift fit for a king because it smelled so good. We also want to give Jesus gifts that are fit for Him. We can offer Him our worship, as well as our lives. I love the old hymn that says, "Give of your best to the Master/Give of the strength of your youth/Throw your fresh burning ardor/Into the battle for truth." ("Give of Your Best to the Master," by Mrs. Charles Barnard. Public domain.) Now, when you are young, serve Jesus with the very best you have!

What's in the Box? A clock

Scripture text: Luke 2:15–19

The point: When the shepherds had seen and worshiped Jesus, they went back to their sheep. Everywhere they went, they shared with others the great news—that Jesus, the Messiah, had been born! They didn't have rich gifts to offer Jesus, but they were able to give others the wonderful gift of knowledge of the Savior. Sharing has been part of the celebration of Christmas ever since that time.

It is now time to share what we have prepared. Last week we prepared some bread (or cookies or candy) to share with others. Tonight we are going to take those homemade gifts to them, just to share some of the wonderful things Jesus has given us.

What's in the Box? Snowflake decoration

Scripture text: Genesis 1:14–19

Special event: Winter solstice (usually December 21)

The point: This is a snowflake, which makes us think of winter. Today marks the first day of winter, or the winter solstice, when the sun shines for the shortest length of time during the day, and it is dark longer than any other night of the year in the Northern Hemisphere. We know that the changes in the length of our days and nights are due to the rotation of the earth around the sun and the "wobble" of the earth on its axis. This agrees with the Bible, which says that among the very first things God created were the sun and the moon to give light and mark the seasons.

Actually, that has nothing to do with Christmas, other than the date we celebrate it. In ancient times, many pagan cultures celebrated the winter solstice because they believed that their god had overcome some evil force that was killing the sun, so the days could get longer once again. Because the Bible does not say when Jesus was born, a custom emerged to celebrate His birth at the same time the pagans were celebrating the winter solstice. This was especially true among Christians who lived where the Roman god Sol Invictus, meaning "the unconquerable sun," was worshiped. The meaning was clear: the Son of God has defeated the unconquerable sun, for Jesus is Lord of all! Over time, of course, the worship of Jesus became almost universal, and Sol Invictus became just an obscure name that we have to look up in some history book!

So, let's enjoy winter, and worship Jesus during this time.

What's in the Box? A manger, or a cow, sheep, or donkey figure

Scripture text: Luke 2:6, 7

The point: This is the week of sharing, so we naturally think about God sharing His Son with us. Because the shepherds shared the good news of Jesus' birth with everyone, we make it a point to share what we have with other people, but there is another bit of sharing we should notice.

The baby was laid in a manger. A manger is a feeding trough for animals— the cattle or donkeys that lived in the stable. They lost their manger for a while! They probably had to give up a warm stall, too, where Mary and Joseph could sleep. Then, they were bothered in the night by shepherds who came looking for the baby.

That's right, the animals in the stable shared with Jesus. That also is a good word for us this Christmas time. The animals shared what they had, and so can we.

What's in the Box? **Card with this "Shepherd Scripture Search" on it**

The point: The shepherds came to Jesus...these texts show God's love for shepherds.

When only two men worshiped God, only one pleased Him.
Who, and why? _____.
Genesis 4:1–4

Moses was the great lawgiver—what was he when God called him?

_____.

Exodus 3:1, 2

David was the great king of Israel, but before he was king, what was he?

_____.

1 Samuel 17:12–15

King David also wrote psalms. His most famous one says the Lord is our _

_____.

Psalm 23:1

Jesus identified Himself in several ways, including the Good

_____.

John 10:10–16

Who does Peter tell to be shepherds of the flock?

_____.

1 Peter 5:1–4

What's in the Box? **A small sack of "crusher–run" or "mill–run" gravel**

Scripture text: 2 Corinthians 6:2

The point: There are many types of gravel, graded according to the size and type of rock, which are useful for various types of concrete work, road work, erosion prevention, and other projects. This particular mix is called "crusher–run," or "mill–run." We sometimes use the expression, "run–of–the–mill," meaning that something is not really special—just quite ordinary. This gravel is like that; it has some larger rock, some smaller, and some medium–sized rock, just a variety of what goes through the crusher every day. It also contains a lot of dust, finely crushed rock that is the by–product of all the other crushing. This type of dust makes "mill–run" good material for building driveways because it all packs together so nicely!

I've noticed there are many big activities we do during Advent: we go to parties, plays, concerts, and the theater; we help the needy with special projects and go on mission trips. These are all good, for many of them make great memories and do much good for others and the kingdom of God. But I have also noticed that many of the best Christmas stories, the ones that really warm our hearts and demonstrate the Spirit of the Christ child, are set during very seemingly ordinary days among everyday surroundings, such as the workplace, home, or in the neighborhood. A small boy saves his allowance to buy something special for a friend, and a blessing comes back to him unexpectedly. A young man makes what he is sure will be a painful visit to an elderly aunt for a cup of tea, and is surprised by joy. Or a simple cobbler helps three people who happen to pass his shop, and entertains the Lord without realizing it.

Sometimes in our "run-of-the-mill" times and places, a very special event happens, and Jesus is very near! When Jesus is near, that is a very special day. That is why our Bible verse says about every day, "this is the day of salvation" or "the time of God's favor." May we all have such a "run-of-the-mill" Christmas!

What's in the Box? **The poem "On the Way to Bethlehem"**
(or write your own poem)

Scripture text: Luke 2:4–7
Special activity: Eat a meal with foods you would take on a trip.

"On the Way to Bethlehem"
By Ben Husted (This may not be good poetry, but it is fun!)

> *Mary and Joseph went a long way*
> *Then ended up sleeping on hay!*
> *They must have traveled many a day;*
> *I wonder, how long did they stay?*
> *Tell me, what did they wear on their feet,*
> *And what did they use for a seat?*

On the road, tell me, what did they eat?
Was it just bread, or was there meat?
No lamb, no turkey, no beef for them
On the long road to Bethlehem.
So tonight we eat just bread with them,
Some nuts, cheese, and grapes on a stem.

The point: Mary and Joseph probably did not have meat for their journey. In that time and place, meat was a luxury, as it still is in many parts of the world. Neither did they have refrigeration nor fast–food restaurants! They probably carried with them some simple foods like whole wheat or barley bread (the staple of their diet), some cheeses, nuts, and dried or fresh fruit. We will join them in eating their simple foods tonight.

What's in the Box? Dirty work gloves

Scripture text: Luke 2:8

The point: These are not the gloves of the rich and influential. They are worn by someone who works with his hands and may get all dirty and smell bad sometimes—someone who could be very much like the shepherds of the Christmas story. Life was hard for shepherds because they were frequently exposed to harsh weather and danger from wild animals and outlaws. They were simple people who led lonely lives, often separated from other people for weeks at a time because they had to watch their sheep every minute of the day. As a result, they could not observe all the details of the Law that would have made them acceptable in much of Jewish society.

On the other hand, these simple people were absolutely essential to society. The animal sacrifices of the Temple could not have been offered up to God without the shepherds. The fellowship meals of the various feasts would have been completely impossible without their provision of the meat. So, even though society may have looked down on shepherds, it was absolutely dependent upon them.

We have people like that today. Migrant farm workers, garbage collectors, road construction workers, and janitors or maids who keep our buildings clean for the rest of society are some of those who come to mind. They are overlooked, but essential.

We are going to take a few minutes to list some of the people like that, then we are going to pray for them. Just as the shepherds are a very big part of the Christmas story, these people also are a very big part of our lives. Let's pray for them and treat them with respect—as friends. Is there someone like this to whom you would like to give a special gift this Christmas?

What's in the Box? A small dove figurine tree decoration

Scripture text: Joel 2:28, 29; Luke 24:49

The point: The dove is a symbol of the Holy Spirit, because when Jesus was baptized by John, he saw the Holy Spirit come upon Jesus in the form of a dove. God had promised through the prophets to send the Holy Spirit not only upon Jesus but upon everyone who would follow Him, even servant girls and slaves. Jesus called this "the promise of my Father." When He had risen from the dead, He told his followers that they would receive the Holy Spirit very soon after He ascended to the Father. That is why we are going to hang this dove on the tree—to remind us that Jesus made it possible to have the Holy Spirit in our lives, making God very real to us.

What's in the Box? A jar of ashes

Scripture text: Leviticus 4:27–31; 5:15,16

The point: We don't think of ashes being associated with Advent, because Jesus' sacrifice makes the burning of offerings on the altar of the temple no longer necessary. When people sinned under the Law of Moses, they were required to bring both a sin offering and a guilt offering to be burned on the altar. The sin offering brought forgiveness—the removal of the record of our sin. The guilt offering brought relief from the subsequent guilt the person felt. These offerings pointed to the coming of the Messiah, the Lamb of God who would take away the sin of the world; this Lamb, Jesus Christ, is both our sin offering and our guilt offering. Our sin is forgiven and our guilt is removed when we simply confess our sin and receive forgiveness. This is the good news that God has shared with us in Jesus.

What's in the Box? **A million dollars in play money**

Scripture text: Proverbs 11:25

Special activity: Watch *It's a Wonderful Life.*

The point: In the movie *It's a Wonderful Life,* George Bailey was always saying, "I wish I had a million dollars", but he never got it. Why? Because he was a man who was always putting other people first, even when he had needs and wants of his own. We all appreciate a person who is generous and helps others, because that is very godlike; God shared Jesus more than generously with us! People who think about others and put their needs above their own are loved, whether they become rich or not. After all his troubles were over, George Bailey saw just how loved he was because he was selfless. Let's watch that movie!

Chapter Four

The Fourth Week:
Angels and Joy

The fourth week in Advent, unlike the other weeks, varies in length from year to year. It may be as short as one day, if Christmas is on Monday, or as long as seven days, if Christmas is on Sunday. This varying length of the week adds a bit of fun, in keeping with its theme of joy. The fourth candle is the Angels' candle, so we have the dual emphases of joy and the angels, which really do seem to go together.

Lighting the Candle
The Sunday before Christmas
The Fourth Sunday in Advent: Angels/Joy
Read Matthew 1:18–25

Christmas is a marvelous story with lots of angels in it! Angels play important roles in almost every part, interacting with almost every character in the story. An angel appeared to Zechariah, the father of John the Baptist, in the temple. The angel Gabriel appeared to Mary. An angel spoke to Joseph in dreams more than once. Also, angels made their spectacular appearance to the shepherds on the night of Jesus' birth.

Angels are spirits who are God's messengers. They speak God's exact word to people and do God's special, powerful acts on behalf of His people. The Scriptures are not always clear about whether God Himself has appeared to a person or whether He has sent an angelic representative. Since angels follow God's exact instructions, however, if an angel appears it is (almost) the same as God appearing Himself.

Even though angels struck terror into the hearts of God's enemies, they also brought the comforting message, "Don't be afraid," to His people. When angels did that, they left His people with an afterglow effect of joy. Think of the relief and joy Joseph must have felt when the angel explained what was going on with Mary. Picture Zechariah's joy at the birth of John the Baptist. Sense the joy of the shepherds. Imagine what joy and excitement Mary must have felt following Gabriel's visit.

Christmas is just days away. Let the joy of the Lord surface in your life! In faith, entrust your worries to Jesus and let the joy of Jesus rise up within you! With joy, light the Angels' candle now.

What's in the Box? **An angel, or Mary from a Nativity scene**

Scripture text: Luke 1:26–38

The point: When an angel suddenly appeared to Mary and spoke to her, she was afraid! Wouldn't you have been? But the angel said, "Don't be afraid." Then he told her about the baby she would have: Jesus, the long–awaited Messiah. As a virgin, she did not see how this could happen, but the angel explained it to her and said, "Nothing is impossible with God." Her answer to all this was: "I am the Lord's servant. May it be to me as you have said." Because of Mary's obedience, what joy was ahead for Mary and for all of us! Nothing is impossible for you, either, so just go ahead and do the will of God! That brings joy.

What's in the Box? **An angel, or Joseph from a Nativity scene**

Scripture text: Matthew 1:18–25

The point: Joseph was afraid to take Mary as his wife, because everyone no doubt assumed her pregnancy was the result of infidelity, as he did. Joseph possibly feared what people would think about him, but we *know* he feared what God thought about the pregnancy. An angel appeared to Joseph in a dream and told him not to be afraid, for this pregnancy was from God. His words brought great comfort and joy for he could take Mary as his wife, knowing that no matter what people thought, he was doing God's will. May God grant that we, too, can do God's will without fear of what people think about us. Then we will have joy.

What's in the Box? An angel, or shepherds from a Nativity scene

Scripture text: Luke 2:8–12

The point: These most humble of people, tending their sheep outside the little town of Bethlehem, did not appear to be good candidates to experience some great revelation of God...but they did! They were terrified! Of course, they were! It was a dark night—a mysterious star shone in the sky and suddenly the angel appeared. Fear gripped them, but the angel quickly said, "Don't be afraid. I bring you great joy."

So we, too, are good candidates to receive some great message from God. We may not be famous or powerful, maybe we're too young or too old, or our job or place in life is too small. But we, just like the shepherds, can come to Jesus and have great joy.

What's in the Box? Dreidel game

Scripture text: John 10:22, 23

Special event: The first day of Hanukkah

The point: This text has the only mention in the Bible of the Feast of Dedication, or Hanukkah. On the Jewish calendar it is the 25th of Kislev, but the date varies on our calendar, usually falling shortly before Christmas. This Jewish holiday is important to us because there would not have been any surviving Jewish people left to bring forth the Messiah without the great deliverance God brought about through the miracle commemorated by this festival.

In a war that ended in 165 BC, Jacob Maccabeus led Israel to its freedom from the evil Greek king, Antiochus Epiphanes. Antiochus had attempted to stamp out the Jewish religion and force the Israelites to adopt Greek culture.

In his unholy zeal, he had defiled the temple with pagan statues and artifacts. Also, historians say that he sacrificed a pig, an unclean animal to the Jews, on the altar. When the victory over this evil sacrilege was won, the Jews cleansed the temple, but when they were ready to light the sacred lamp, inside they found only enough sacred oil for one day's burning. They lit the lamp anyway, and God multiplied the oil so the lamp burned for eight days, until more sacred oil was found. The remembrance of this miracle has now been a Jewish festival for two thousand years, and we see from our text that Jesus was in the temple for its celebration.

The central item in this festival is the Menorah, a candleholder with nine candles—one for the sacred lamp and one for each of the eight days it burned with the miraculous oil. This is the first day of the eight–day Hanukkah festival, and in Jewish homes tonight two candles are lit, with the central candle representing the sacred lamp and the other the first day's burning. On the second day, three are lit, and so on until the eighth day when the Menorah glows with all its candles burning.

The dreidel game is a Hanukkah tradition. To play, each person antes up something into the pot, often chocolate gelt (coins). Then the first player spins the dreidel, a four–sided top. When it stops, the letter on the top–most side determines the next step for that player. When the pot is empty, the game is over. These are the letters on the sides of the dreidel and what they mean in the game: Nun = nothing happens and the next player spins. Gimel = the player wins the pot. Heh = the player wins half the pot. Shin = the player must match the pot. These letters are the first letters of the Hebrew words standing for "a great miracle happened there."

The top can be made out of clay, or you can make it out of paper or cardboard with a short dowel rod for a spinner. The actual Hebrew letters are listed below.

Let's play a few rounds!

ן	Nun	Nothing happens and the next player spins.
ג	Gimel	The player wins the pot.
ה	Heh	The player wins half the pot.
ש	Shin	The player must match the pot.

For more information on Hanukkah and the dreidel, go to www.hanukkah–traditions.com.

What's in the Box? A pocket New Testament and two small cups

Scripture text: Revelation 14:6–12

The point: Angels had much to do with the preparation for the first coming of Jesus. This text tells us they also have much to do to get ready for His second coming as well.

In this text, the first angel proclaims the eternal gospel. Exactly what this means is not clear. Does this angel go out at some future time to directly proclaim the gospel in such a way that humans can hear the angel speak? Or is this simply indicating angelic activity directing and empowering people as they proclaim the gospel? The text doesn't say. At any rate, the gospel is proclaimed, and that always produces joy for those who receive it! That is why there is a New Testament, often called "the gospel," in the box today.

The second and third angels speak of two cups, so there are two cups in the box along with the gospel. These cups add a very serious note to our celebration.

The second angel proclaims the fall of Babylon the Great which caused all nations to drink from her cup of adulteries. This cup has a spiritual power that entraps peoples and nations in sin, but it will be destroyed in the last days and the cup will be dashed from the hand of Babylon the Great. There will be great joy among those who have been freed from slavery when that demonic power is broken by God's judgment falling upon it.

The third angel says that the cup of the wrath of God will be poured out upon those who have bought into Babylon's deception and taken the Mark of the Beast. These who have willfully joined in the sadistic and demonic attacks upon all righteousness and the followers of Jesus will suffer in the end what their choices and actions deserve. When they are reaping what they have sown and are no longer tormenting the just, there will be great joy!

The Gospel and two cups: there will be judgment and there will be joy at the second Advent of Jesus.

What's in the Box? **Scrabble tiles spelling "JOY."**

Scripture text: Matthew 2:10; Luke 1:41, 46–47, 58; 2:10

The point: Jesus intends for us to have fun and enjoy life, especially at Christmas. We find references to joy and rejoicing in the Christmas story. There is even mention of John the Baptist "leaping" in the womb of Elizabeth when Mary, the mother of Jesus, entered the house. The angel told the shepherds, "I bring you tidings of great joy."

Tonight we are going to do something just for fun: playing some board games. First, we are going to play Guesstures with some new cards—each with a word connected to Christmas. Then we are going to play Scrabble, but our rules have changed a bit for tonight. We can use words from other languages and capitalized words, as long as they have to do with Christmas. Any time we use a word having to do with Christmas, the points earned for that word are doubled. (Adapt other games of your choice.)

What's in the Box? **Mouse and cheese ornament**

Scripture text: Revelation 19:9, 10

The point: Oh, mouse and cheese! We are going to read a pretend story about what happened on Christmas Eve when not even a mouse was stirring in the house. We have already read the story about the real Saint Nicholas, who loved and worshiped Jesus very much, just as our Scripture text tells us, too. Now we are going to read the entirely pretend story about Santa Claus that so many people believe. Clement Moore wrote this wonderful poem, which popularized the image of Santa with his red suit, jolly belly, and reindeer. We worship Jesus, not this made–up Santa, but we are going to read this poem and just have fun! (Read *The Night Before Christmas*.)

What's in the Box? **A snowflake or a package of fake snow**

Scripture text: Job 37:5, 6

Special activity: This is the week of the Angel candle and it snowed, so let's go make snow angels!

What's in the Box? A colorful Christmas light bulb

Scripture text: John 8:12

Special activity: Because Jesus is the Light of the world, we have decorated our house. Other people have, too, making the houses in the neighborhood look beautiful. So, tonight we are going to get in our car to drive around and look at those lights.

What's in the Box? A candle

Scripture text: Nehemiah 8:10

Special activity: Eat a meal by candlelight, and then blow out the candles.

The point: The joy of the Lord is your strength. Having the joy of Jesus in our hearts gives us a strength that other people don't have, and when we share it that helps other people, too. What if our family was the only one around this area with Jesus and that joy? Would that help much? What if we have only our Advent candles burning in a room; will they help very much? We are going to find out. We are going to eat our meal tonight with only our candles for lighting. Then we are going to blow the candles out and just see what a difference that makes.

What's in the Box? A crown

Scripture text: Revelation 4

The point: Some people really get to wear crowns here on earth. There are kings and emperors, though we don't have those in this country. We think of crowns placed on the heads of homecoming queens or Miss America. But in the time that Jesus was born, a crown was a very important thing, because it represented royalty, power and the authority to rule over people. Also, Jesus said some of his followers would sit on thrones in heaven and rule. Then the apostle John was shown this picture of what actually happens in heaven.

At the very center of all the splendor of heaven there is a great throne, around which are twenty–four other thrones. Those who are sitting upon those thrones wearing crowns are those of whom Jesus spoke as ruling in heaven. There are also four living creatures who are closer to the throne than the twenty–four elders, and from time to time they give glory, honor, and thanks to the One who sits on the throne. When that happens, the twenty–four elders bow down and lay their crowns before the One on the throne.

While we are on earth we may never get a crown, but we may very well get a trophy, a plaque, or a certificate saying, "You did well!" We might get lots of money and have lots of power and influence in business, school, or church. In heaven, all these things are laid before the throne, for God is absolutely much greater than we are, no matter what we may have become. In heaven, all the angels and the people are praising God and enjoying His presence. That is the right thing for us to do here on earth, too.

So, we are going to put this little crown here by the Christ candle on our wreath so that we are always reminded to give glory to Jesus, our King of kings.

What's in the Box? Matchbox car

Scripture text: Luke 2:1–5

The point: Joseph and Mary went "home" for that first Christmas, when Jesus was born. They went there because Bethlehem was Joseph's ancestral home. People have been going to see their families for Christmas ever since. That's what we're doing tomorrow. We're going to load up in our car and go to Grandma and Grandpa's house for Christmas!

What's in the Box? A small, gift–wrapped box or wood block (for Christmas Eve)

Scripture text: Matthew 2:11

Special event: Opening the Christmas gifts on Christmas Eve

The point: The Wise Men gave gifts to Jesus to express their love for Him—God's greatest Gift! Because God has given us the greatest Gift we could ever receive—Jesus Christ—we also have prepared to give gifts to those we love. So, let's go open the gifts we are giving each other!

Christmas Eve
Lighting the Christ Candle
Read Matthew 1:18–2:12

We have come to the end of the Advent season. We have planned, prepared, shared, and sensed joy. We now proclaim that Jesus Christ is come!

For children—and for adults—Christmas Eve is also the end of the long wait to see what are in those packages under the tree. Guessing, wishing, and maybe shaking them will soon give way to knowledge and joy. We will have great fun, and life will never be quite the same again because of what we give and receive.

So it is with Christ. When we have received Him, nothing is ever the same again. Life is forever different, and we get the very most out of life when we keep Him at life's center. The Christ candle stands in the center of the wreath. Light it now, with a prayer to keep Jesus in the center of your life.

PART THREE:

The Appendices

APPENDIX ONE
Stories We Have Read

These are stories we have used in the Advent box. We have torn most of them out of magazines and kept them over the years; these we just fold up and put behind one of the doors of the box. Some are in books that are too large to fit in the box; with these, we put some object in the box representing the story. Since we open our box at mealtime, when we find a story in the box we set it aside to be read after the meal, rather than keeping the children (or Dad) waiting to eat.

We have spent about twenty-five years collecting stories. Some years we find none that we want to keep, but other years we find several. You will want to make your own collection by reading the stories in various magazines every Christmas. Many magazines have new stories every year, some of which you will find "dumb," or "silly," or just not your style; we certainly have read many of those! Then again, sometimes you will find a story you consider well-written, full of good Christian content, and personally touching! Hang on to the good ones; they may find their way into your box year after year. Some of the following stories are read every year in our home, and they are most important. The Advent box is all about bringing the family closer together around Christ, and traditions—activities done every year—are the glue!

Buck, Pearl S. "Christmas Day in the Morning." In *A Family Christmas, Reader's Digest*. Pleasantville, NY: Readers Digest Association, 1984. A fifteen–year–old boy discovers the real joy of giving.

Burns, Thomas J. "The Second Greatest Christmas Story Ever Told." In December, 1989 issue of *Reader's Digest*. How Charles Dickens wrote *A Christmas Carol* is a tremendous story in itself. It is a tale of a talented man giving his talent to enrich the joy of others.

Degi, Joseph. "Christmas, 1944."In December, 1988 issue of *Guideposts*. A group of Seabees in the jungles of New Guinea have a large group of barely clad native men appear at their camp on Christmas Eve—and sing Christmas carols in their own language, but to familiar tunes.

Donohue, Dina. "Trouble at the Inn." Originally in December, 1966 issue of *Guideposts*; reprinted in December, 2004. In this classic story, a nine–year–old boy, by his compassionate outburst, ruins the Christmas pageant—or does he?

Fish, Will. "For Always." In *Cross Talk Ministries Newsletter*, December 19, 1998. A small Russian orphan makes a manger with two babies in it.

Fison, David. "An Order I Couldn't Refuse." In December, 2000 issue of *Guideposts*. Christmas aboard a troop ship, taking the wounded home from New Guinea in 1944.

Frankel, Stanley A. "The Story Behind Rudolph the Red–Nosed Reindeer." In *Good Housekeeping*, December, 1989, page 126. Rudolph, one of the most recognizable parts of the modern Christmas fable, is not something we want in our box! But we want our children to understand where he came from. The story of his creation has qualities that the poem itself almost misses.

Gordon, Arthur. "The Legend of the First Crèche." In the 1981 *Guideposts* Christmas Card. A heartwarming legend about St. Francis of Assisi.

Holmes, Jean. "Caleb the Camel." Illustrated by Chuck Reasoner. In Nov/Dec issue of *Virtue Magazine*, 1980. A fun pretend story about a camel who may have carried one of the Wise Men to Jesus!

Kay, Ellie. "Remember Your Shoes." In *Focus on the Family*, December, 2002. God teaches a busy mom about priorities through a six-year-old not wearing his shoes.

Lambert, David. "My Dumb Sister and the Crazy Shepherds." In Nov/Dec 1982 issue of *Virtue Magazine*. A boy has to take his little sister to the mall to shop, where she gets lost and ends up kneeling at the manger scene where a choir is singing. It makes Christmas real for everyone in the mall.

Matthews, Dianne. "The Perfect Gift." In *Focus on the Family*,

December 2000. A five-year-old girl steals an empty Christmas present and gets a life lesson.

McCain, John. "Joyful and Triumphant." In December, 1984 issue of *Reader's Digest*. The story of John McCain and his fellow POWs celebrating Christmas in a North Vietnamese prison.

O. Henry. "The Gift of the Magi." In *The Saturday Evening Christmas Treasury*, Bonanza Books, 1986. Originally published in two volumes, with this story in the first, *The Saturday Evening Post Christmas Book*, Curtis Publishing Company, 1976. A classic story with a surprise ending of a husband and wife who sell their most precious possessions to give the other their best Christmas present.

Oursler, Fulton. "A String of Blue Beads." In the 1979 Guideposts Christmas Card. Pleasantville, NY: Reader's Digest Association, 1951. From the book published by Doubleday & Co. A grief–stricken shopkeeper finds life again as he lets a little girl buy a string of expensive turquoise beads for pennies.

Powers, Mala. "On the Way to Christmas." In December 1978 issue of *Guideposts*. The original inspiration for our Advent box.

Rayner, Diane. "Night of Wonder." In the November/December, 1989 issue of *The Christian Reader*. Reprinted from December, 1983 issue of *Guideposts*. A small boy saves for months to buy his best friend a special Christmas gift. For his effort he gets a nasty shock and burn, then a miracle of healing!

Schade, Howard C. "The Gold and Ivory Tablecloth." In *Focus on the Family*, December 1999, reprinted with permission from *Reader's Digest*, December, 1954. From the book, *A Match Made in Heaven*, Susan Wales and Ann Platz, eds. Oregon: Multnomah Publishers, 1999. An immigrant husband and wife, who presumed each other killed in Hitler's Germany, are reunited on Christmas Eve through a unique tablecloth bought by a pastor for almost nothing at a benefit auction.

Sherrill, Elizabeth. "Christmas, 1818." In December 1988 issue of *Guideposts*. The reason why "Silent Night" was written for the guitar rather than the organ.

Tolstoy, Leo. "Where Love Is, God Is." From *Twenty–Three Tales*, English translation by Louise and Aylmer Maude, Oxford University Press. Condensed by *Reader's Digest*, December, 1982. This is one of our very favorite stories, and it is in the box every year! A Russian cobbler is shown the meaning of, "As you have done it unto the least of these..."

Williams, Jeannie. "Where's the Baby Jesus?" In November/December, 1986 issue of *Good News*. The story of why the author keeps a Nativity scene without the baby Jesus in it.

APPENDIX TWO
Books We Have Read

Just like the stories above, some of these books are read at our house every year. Some of them are very old but still in print, while others can be found in recent publications. Judy, especially, is always on the lookout for well–written, well–illustrated books to add to our collection. She is credited with finding *Mr. Toomey* and *A Cup of Christmas Tea* for us.

For small children, the best place to find stories and books is in the children's section of your local Christian bookstores. The Christmas story is told creatively for children with fun pictures in many small books like *Simeon's Secret*, which I have listed below.

Of course, these books do not fit in the box. So, we use some small object to put in the box that reminds us of that book. We use a wood chisel to tell us to read *Mr. Toomey* and a Dickens Christmas tree ornament to represent *A Christmas Carol.*

As with the stories, we read the book after the meal. Some of these books can be read in one sitting, while others have to be read over the course of a few days. Undoubtedly, you will enjoy reading them aloud with the entire family present!

Dickens, Charles. *A Christmas Carol.* New York: Bantam Classics, 1986. First published in 1843, this little book is still in print. You can find it in many new and used bookstores at very little cost. This is the marvelous tale of the transformation of Ebenezer Scrooge! While not an evangelical tract, this famous story has much excellent Christian content.

Walt Disney Productions. *Mickey's Christmas Carol,* a Little Golden Book. New York: Golden Press, 1983. If your children aren't ready for Dickens' original, this is a fun and creative story adapted by Walt Disney. Rebekah still insists that we have to read this little book and watch the video every year!

Dobson, James, ed. *A Family Christmas.* Illustrated by G. Harvey. Oregon: Multnomah Press, 2002. A beautifully written and illustrated collection of Christmas stories to warm the heart.

Garner, James Finn. *Politically Correct Holiday Stories.* New York: Macmillan, 1995. I used this book one year when only seventeen–year–old Rebekah was still at home, with a note in the box saying, "Be glad God is in charge of Christmas!" The book is a spoof of extreme political correctness and what it might do to some of our favorite Christmas stories.

Hegg, Tom. *A Cup of Christmas Tea.* Illustrated by Warren Hanson. Minneapolis, MN: Waldman House Press, Inc., 1982. An emotionally moving story in poetry form of a busy young man who grudgingly takes time out to visit an elderly great aunt, and is warmed by more than the cup of tea.

Holmes, Marjorie. *Two From Galilee.* New York: Bantam Books in conjunction with Fleming H. Revell Company, 1972. An imaginative and well–written historical novel about Mary and Joseph.

Kramer, Janice. *Simeon's Secret.* Iillustrated by Betty Wind. St. Louis, Missouri: Concordia, 1969. A children's story of how it might really have been for Simeon, the prophet in the temple who blesses the baby Jesus in Luke's gospel. We wore the cover entirely off this one!

Myra, Harold. *Santa Are You For Real?* Illustrated by Dwight Walles. New York: Thomas Nelson Inc.,1977. This was an incredibly helpful book to us, for it describes the origin of Santa as St. Nicholas of Myra in a tasteful way. Well–written and beautifully illustrated, it is great for reading to small children.

Robinson, Barbara. *The Best Christmas Pageant Ever*. New York: Avon Books, 1972. A hilarious book about a Christmas pageant ruined, or perfected, by a "bad" family. This book is still in print for a good reason; it is good!

Wojciechowski, Susan. *The Christmas Miracle of Jonathan Toomey*. Illustrated by P.J. Lynch. Cambridge, Massachusetts: Candlewick Press, 1995. This great story about the power of love to bring about change can be read in one sitting to children of all ages.

APPENDIX THREE

Bible Texts to Help With Your Devotions

The Revised Common Lectionary (1992)

The following list of Scriptures needs some introduction for many of us. Advent is, as we have said, part of the tradition of the church as the first season of the church year. As churches worshiped year after year, they often used the same Scriptures again and again, while some texts of great value for public reading, teaching, and preaching were lost. So, various individuals and groups made a point of collecting lists of Scriptures that could be used in the various seasons—texts not to be forgotten.

One recent step in this process resulted in "The Revised Common Lectionary (1992)," which various denominations then adapted to their own purposes. The following list for Advent is used by permission of the Consultation on Common Texts. This is a list of various texts for public worship, arranged to be read in a three–year cycle (YEARS A, B, and C). Unless you belong to a Christian tradition that has strict guidelines on the lectionary's use, you are free to utilize the list however the Holy Spirit leads you in your own home.

Year A	Year B	Year C
First Sunday in Advent		
Isaiah 2:1–5	Isaiah 64:1–9	Jeremiah 33:14–16
Psalm 12	2Psalm 80:1–7, 17–19	Psalm 25:1–10
Romans 13:11–141	Corinthians 1:3–91	Thess. 3:9–13
Matthew 24:36–44	Mark 13:24–37	Luke 21:25–36
Second Sunday in Advent		
Isaiah 11:1–10	Isaiah 40:1–11	Malachi 3:1–4
Psalm 72:1–7, 18, 19	Psalm 85:1–2, 8–13	Luke 1:68–79
Romans 15:4–13	2 Peter 3:8–15a	Philippians 1:3–11
Matthew 3:1–12	Mark 1:1–8	Luke 3:1–6
Third Sunday in Advent		
Isaiah 35:1–10	Isaiah 61:1–4, 8–11	Zephaniah 3:14–20
Luke 1:47–55	Psalm 126	Isaiah 12:2–6
James 5:7–10	1 Thessalonians 5:16–24	Philippians 4:4–7
Matthew 11:2–11	John 1:6–8, 19–28	Luke 3:7–18
Fourth Sunday in Advent		
Isaiah 7:10–16	2 Samuel 7:1–11, 16	Micah 5:2–5a
Psalm 80:1–7, 17–19	Luke 1:47–55	Luke 1:47–55
Romans 1:1–7	Romans 16:25–27	Hebrews 10:5–10
Matthew 1:18–25	Luke 1:26–38Luke 1:39–45	

Our List of Advent Scriptures

Over a period of ten or twelve years, our family hosted an Advent Open House on the first Sunday in Advent. We lived in church–owned parsonages during those years, and our Open House was a way to thank everyone for their kindness to us and to let them see how we were caring for the parsonage.

Each year we prepared cookies of many kinds, hot chocolate and hot apple cider, and cheeses and crackers of many kinds. We also gave each family that attended a handmade gift. One year we made more than fifty Advent wreaths like ours and gave one to each family, along with a devotion booklet we had prepared. The booklet included devotions for the Sundays and Christmas Eve to go with the lighting of each candle and a suggested Scripture passage to be read on the other days of each week. The list in that booklet is reproduced below, to which I have added other passages appropriate for the week. This is not an exhaustive list—just a place to begin.

Week One	Week Two	Week Three	Week Four
Prophecy	Bethlehem	Shepherds	Angels
Planning	Preparation	Sharing	Joy
Isaiah 2:1–5	Micah 5:2–4	Luke 2:17	Luke 2:8–14
Isaiah 11:1–10	Luke 1:26–38	Luke 2:8–20	Matt. 1:18–25
Luke 1:5–25	Isaiah 40:1–11	Ezek. 34:11–24	Matt. 2:1–12
Luke 1:57–66	Micah 4:1–7	John 10:1–15,27	Matt. 2:13–15
Luke 1:67–80	Malachi 3:1–7	1 Peter 2:21–25	Luke 1:8–20
1 Thess. 4:13–18	Matt.1:1–17	Psalm 23	Luke 1:26–38
1 Thess. 5:1–3	John 14:2	Luke 1:26–37	Luke 1:39–45
1 Cor. 1:3–9	Rom. 15:4–13	Luke 1:39–56	Luke 1:46–55
John 3:14–21	1 Thess. 5:4–11	Rev. 5:1–14	John 16:19–24
John 14:1–7	Rev. 21:5–8	1 Peter 5:1–4	Rev. 22:1–7
Rev. 22:12–16	Matt. 3	Matt. 28:16–20	Isaiah 51:11
Isaiah 14:24–27	Eph. 2:8–10	Heb. 13:15, 16	Psalm 126
Jeremiah 33:14–18	2 Peter 3:8–14	Isaiah 35:1–10	Isaiah 7:10–17
Isaiah 64:1–8	Mark 1:1–8	Isaiah 61:1–3,10–11	2 Sam. 7:1–16
Luke 21:25–36	Luke 3:1–6	Zeph. 3:14–18a	Heb 10:5–10

Appendix Four
Other Advent Traditions

As I have said, we made our choice of the meaning of the weeks and the colors of the candles from a variety of traditions. As far as we can tell, none of these traditions is right or wrong; they just originated and developed in different areas. Here are a few of the others. Again, unless you are from a Christian tradition with strict guidelines concerning liturgical colors, you are free to choose for yourself.

Regarding the colors of the candles, we found at least four variations:

- Four white candles and one red candle as the Christ candle
- Four red candles and a white Christ candle
- Four purple candles (the liturgical color of Advent) and a white Christ candle
- Three purple candles and a rose candle (Third Sunday), with a white Christ candle

We did not find any particular significance to the colors, except in the tradition of using three purple candles and one rose candle. In that case, the three purple candles signify penitence, and the rose candle represented joy. This tradition appears to come from seventh century Gaul, where Advent was a season of fasting among the monks broken only on the third Sunday, "Guadete Sunday." (Gaudete means "Rejoice ye!")

At the time we started exploring this subject, I knew some in liturgical circles who insisted that this last mentioned arrangement was the "proper" way to celebrate Advent. However, as we prayed about it and studied all we could find, we could find no reason why that particular tradition should be the only one. What I could not understand then, and cannot yet today, is why Advent should be marked by penitence and fasting. I certainly have nothing against repentance or fasting, and have practiced both very often, but I cannot understand why the season in preparation for Christmas should be a time of mourning over sin. So, we decided to adopt another tradition which seemed to have at least an equal claim to validity: four red candles and a white Christ candle.

The four weeks of the season were given various meanings as well, such as:

- First Sunday: Christ's coming in final victory
- Second Sunday: John the Baptist
- Third Sunday: Also John the Baptist
- Fourth Sunday: The events immediately preceding the birth of Christ.

Or these:

- First Sunday: Anticipation and longing
- Second Sunday: Preparation for the coming Christ
- Third Sunday: Rejoicing in anticipation
- Fourth Sunday: God's great gift of love and hope.

We found more support and appreciation for the tradition we adopted:

- First Sunday: The Prophecy candle, with a theme of planning
- Second Sunday: The Bethlehem candle, with a theme of preparation
- Third Sunday: The Shepherds' candle, with a theme of sharing
- Fourth Sunday: The Angels' candle, with the theme of joy

Appendix Five
The Church Year

Here is a quick look at the church year as commonly observed now, for your reference.

The Season of Advent

- Advent means "coming," for the first and second coming of Jesus
- Begins the fourth Sunday before Christmas day
- Ends Christmas Eve
- Varies from twenty–two to twenty–eight days

The Season of Christmastide

- Begins with Christmas Day
- The famous twelve days of Christmas

The Season of Epiphany

- Epiphany means "revealing"
- Commemorates the Wise Men's visit or the Lord's baptism by John
- Begins on the Day of Epiphany, January 6

The Season of Lent

- A period of forty days plus Sundays preceding Easter Day
- Begins on Ash Wednesday
- A time of fasting and prayer in preparation for Easter

The Season of Eastertide

- Begins Easter Day
- Celebrates the resurrection of Jesus

The Season of Pentecost

- Begins on the Day of Pentecost, fifty days after Easter
- Celebrates the giving of the Holy Spirit and His work in us
- Continues until the beginning of Advent, in most traditions

The Season of Kingdomtide

- Is contained in some recent traditions, but not in all
- Begins the last Sunday in August
- Commemorates growth of the Kingdom of God
- Ends with the beginning of Advent

APPENDIX SIX
Building an Advent Wreath or Box

The Advent Wreath

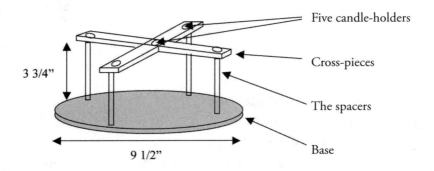

Five candle-holders

Cross-pieces

The spacers

Base

3 3/4"

9 1/2"

1. Cut the base from ¾" plywood, a circle of 9½" diameter.
2. Cut the cross–pieces from 1 x 2 lumber, 9½" in length.
3. Notch the top pieces, glue and fit together; clamp until glue cures.
4. Clamp the cross–pieces to the base and drill pilot holes, centered and ¾" from the ends, for the candle holes and dowel rods, with a ⅛" bit, through the top pieces into the base.

5. Drill the dowel holes ¼" in diameter and ⅛" deep in top pieces, ¼" in diameter and ⅜" deep in the base.

6. Drill the five ¾" diameter candle holes in the top pieces, ⅜" deep.

7. Cut the dowel rods 4¼" long and fit the whole thing together, with glue.

8. Stain and finish as desired.

The Advent Box
Figure One-Front View

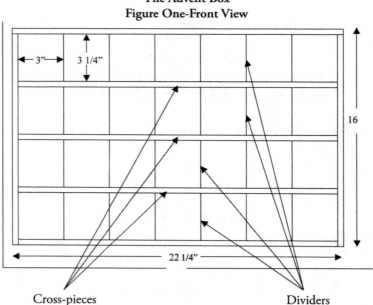

Cross-pieces   Dividers

1. Cut two sides 7 ¼" x ¾" x 16" long.

2. Cut the top 7¼" x ¾" x 22¼" long.

3. Cut the bottom 7¼" x ¾" x 21" long.

4. Cut the three cross–pieces 7" x ¾" x 21" long. These are ¼" narrower than the top, bottom and sides, allowing the plywood back to be inset.

5. Cut the grooves in the sides ⅛" deep to inset the bottom and cross pieces. See Figure Two. Note that the sides must be mirror images of each other.

6. Cut a groove along the full length of each side, on the front–inside edge ⅛" x ⅜" to allow the doors to inset slightly.

7. Cut a groove on the back-inside edge of each side ¼" x ¼" for the back to be inset.

Figure Two—Groove Placement for Sides
All grooves ⅛" deep

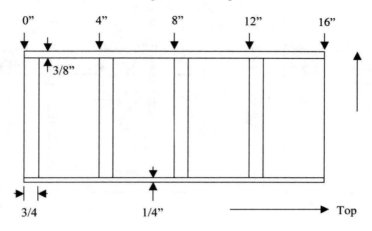

8. Cut 28 doors 2 15/16'" x 3 3/16" x ⅜" thick, with the grain vertical. and all edges well. (Two coats of polyurethane finish may make the doors too snug.)

9. Cut a groove along the back–inside edge of the bottom ¼" x ¼" to inset the back.

10. Cut a groove along the back–inside edge of the top ¼" x ¼", ending at ½" from each end for the back inset.

11. Cut the back from ¼" plywood 15 ¾"x 21 ¼" wide.

12. Cut grooves in top side of bottom, and both sides of cross–pieces ¼" x ⅛" to inset dividers. Grooves may reach only to within ⅜" of front. Grooves must be every 3" on center from each end.

Figure Three – Groove Placement in Cross–Pieces

All grooves ⅛" deep

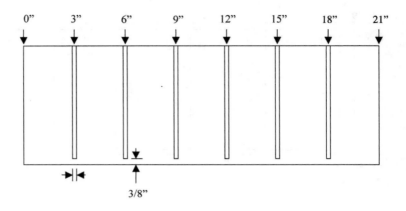

13. Groove placement for the bottom is identical with that of the cross–pieces, but there is a ¼" x ¼" groove along the back to inset the plywood back. The top is a mirror image of the bottom, except that it is 5/8" longer on both ends.

14. Cut 24 dividers from ¼" plywood, 6 ¾" x 3 ½". Sand all edges well so the dividers will slide into their slots.

15. Assemble the frame: top, sides, bottom, and cross–pieces, using glue and the fasteners of your choice—finish nails, screws, biscuits, or dowel pins.

16. Apply a small amount of glue and slide dividers into their slots, making sure they are fully inserted so they will act as the doorstops and not interfere with the back.

Figure Four—Door Details

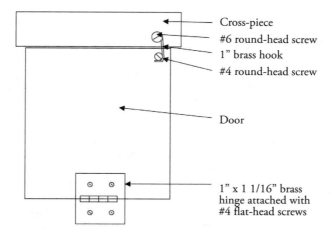

Cross-piece
#6 round-head screw
1" brass hook
#4 round-head screw

Door

1" x 1 1/16" brass
hinge attached with
#4 flat-head screws

17. Apply stain and one coat of clear finish to all surfaces except the groove where the back will be installed; glue will not adhere to finished wood. It will be very difficult to stain and finish the interior after the back is installed.

18. Set the doors of one row in place, with uniform spaces between them. (Two business cards is about 1/32" thick.) Carefully place the hinges on them, using a straight edge to keep them in line; drill pilot holes and attach hinges to the cross–piece.

19. Then drill pilot holes and attach the hinges to the doors, being careful to keep the spaces between them uniform.

20. Remove doors. Keeping them in order, stain them and apply two coats of finish.

21. Stain the back and apply a coat of finish. Glue and nail it in place.

22. Apply a second coat of finish to the box exterior.

23. Re–attach the doors. Install the latches.